The Ghosts of Brooklyn

Thrilling Accounts of Souls, Spirits and Ghosts

L. V. Salazar

ATTENTION CORPORATIONS, UNIVERSITIES, COLLEGES, AND PROFESSIONAL AND CHARITABLE ORGANIZATIONS: Quantity discounts are available on bulk purchases of this book for educational and gift purposes, or as premiums in fundraising efforts. Inquiries should be sent to

nfo@hispaniceconomics.com.

Hispanic Economics, Inc.

P.O. Box 140681

Coral Gables, FL 33114-0681

info@hispaniceconomics.com

HispanicEconomics.com

ISBN 978-0-9791176-2-6

Cover and Interior Design by John Clifton

john@johnclifton.net

For Marty Markowitz

Whose soul is the essence of Brooklyn

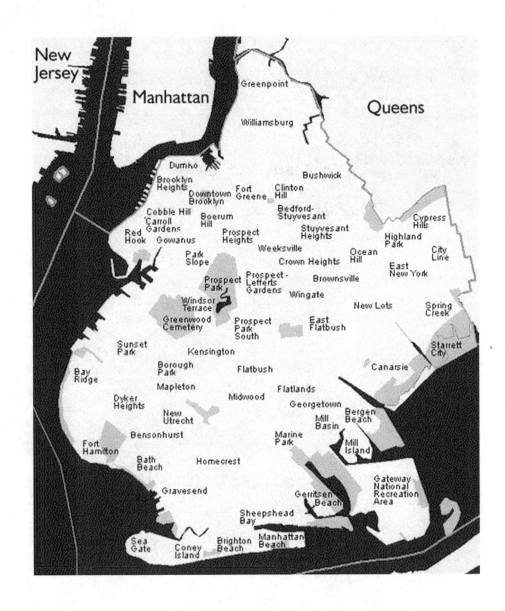

The Neighborhoods of Brooklyn, NY
(Detailed maps on Page 78)

✠ Table of Contents ✠

✠ Introduction ✠

A few years ago a friend from Oaxaca opened a restaurant in Park Slope. It featured the regional cooking of his home state in Mexico. He proudly showcased the place as a "Oaxacan kitchen." It specialized in the chocolate-infused sauces known as *mole*, and other delicacies, such as toasted grasshoppers. (Think of popcorn, with legs.) It was noted in the *New York Times* as part of Brooklyn's emerging restaurant scene.

The restaurant was located on 7th Avenue near Lincoln Place. On the several occasions I went over with friends, the conversation turned to the "ghost" that haunted the area. I knew nothing about it. But I was told that a woman, dressed in a white gown—was it a sleeping gown or a hospital gown?—"haunted" the area around Carroll Street and 6th Avenue. She would be seen clutching her rib cage, as if she had a stomach ache. Or as if she had been shot. There was disagreement on this point. But there was a consensus that she was there and she was real.

A ghost. A haunting. Really?

It was a story, an urban legend, easy to dismiss.

That is, of course, until one evening when, standing on the corner waiting for the light to change, a different friend repeated the story of the ghost clutching her rib cage. I rolled my eyes. An older woman, who had been standing nearby and

When two or more individuals report seeing a ghost, or there are consistent stories about ghosts in a specific place, the next questions become: Who was this apparition in life? Is it possible to find out their name?

overheard us, then spoke up.

"Not only is she real," she said. "But she has a name. Mrs. Osborne. My grandmother knew her in life. This was back during World War I. You can look it up if you don't believe me! It's Mrs. Osborne, and this is her neighborhood."

The light changed, and we went our separate ways.

You can look it up. Was this a joke, or a challenge?

The fact that you are reading this book means I took it as a challenge.

This project began a couple of years ago, in an informal manner, and one that paralleled a similar project investigating paranormal

activity in the Yucatan with the guidance of a Maya H'men, which is a traditional healer or shaman. When two or more individuals report seeing a ghost, or there are consistent stories about ghosts in a specific place, the next questions become: Who was this apparition in life? Is it possible to find out their name? Once that is known, what other material facts can be uncovered? In other words, is there anything to substantiate the reported nature of this haunting?

Who was this Mrs. Osborne who is seen wandering near Carroll Street and 6th Avenue in Park Slope?

Her story is told later on. For now, the following information will suffice. Mrs. Julia Osborne, lived off Carroll Street and 6th Avenue, and was a parishioner of the Old First Reformed Church located at 729 Carroll Street for almost half a century. The era in question dated from the time before the Civil War until her death in 1918. She died of an unexplained hemorrhage of the pancreas. Today, it is said she does not realize she is dead, but simply is wandering the streets waiting for church services to begin. She is said to clutch her rib cage because she does not know she is hemorrhaging blood.

In the lore of the neighborhood, she is known to old timers, Park Slope residents who have lived there for decades. The apparition is a new phenomenon for young families and urban professionals moving into the neighborhood. But her

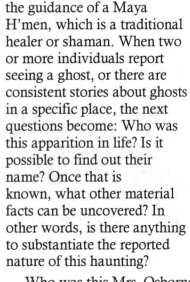

presence is being sensed by newcomers in due course. The family that owned the Oaxacan kitchen, not unlike many indigenous peoples throughout our hemisphere, is culturally more in tune with a "sixth sense" about the presence of the paranormal in our lives. They confirmed the "exuberant" number of ghosts and spirits that live in this area of Brooklyn. It is not surprising when so many Brooklynites have met untimely deaths—from the Civil War to the Great Theater Fire of 1876, from World War I to the 9/11 terrorist attack on New York.

This book compiles 36 of the more intriguing ghost stories. It is hoped that the reader will take pleasure learning about both the haunted places and the stories of the lives these ghosts lived. Take a look around, and see if you can sense their presence. Delight in the effervescence and vitality of these unexpected neighbors. Recognize and honor the continuity they offer acro ages. There is something to said for the paranormal liveliness in our midst, particularly given the abundance of the abnormal we have to endure by choosing to live in this exasperating, frustrating, wonderful and magnificent city.

Here's to you, Mrs. Osborne.

L. V. Salazar
Brooklyn, NY

Author's Notes

When this project began in 2009 there were only a handful of verified ghost stories in Brooklyn. Most notably is the Melrose Hall ghost of Alva and, of course, the ghost of the missing child believed to haunt the Brooklyn Public Library. Since then scores of other stories have surfaced. This book contains the first 36 stories that have been authenticated to the satisfaction of this writer.

There are, however, more than 350 paranormal investigations under way. In consequence, there will be a subsequent book of confirmed ghost stories. Indeed, as this goes to press, an additional 36 stories are under final review.

Readers are invited to participate. Got Brooklyn ghost leads? If you do, send them to: ParanormalBrooklyn@gmail.com.

Please be advised all biblical quotations are from the King James Bible.

The Ghost of the Boy Who Fell from the Sky sits on these steps of the 78th Police Precinct, at 65 6th Avenue, Brooklyn, New York.

Brooklyn Heights ✠

The Spirit of Augustin Vigil

I t is one of the more intriguing spirits that wanders the streets of Brooklyn. In life, his name was Augustín Vigil, and he was born in Havana, Cuba. He emigrated to the United States and enlisted in the 39th New York Volunteer Infantry Regiment. He fought on the side of the Union in the Civil War. He died at the Union Hotel General Hospital in Georgetown, Washington, D.C. He was 20.

The official cause of death was pulmonary tuberculosis. This was a familiar cause of death during the Civil War.

Private Vigil did not really die of pulmonary tuberculosis, however. He died of malnutrition. During the summer of 1861—Private Vigil died July 8, 1861—there was a critical shortage of food at the hospitals around Washington, D.C. treating the Civil War injured. The 39th New York Volunteer Infantry Regiment consisted of many Latin Americans who, emboldened by the

The spirit of Augustín Vigil appears, walking across the Brooklyn Bridge from Manhattan. He makes his way to Hicks Street until he reaches Grace Court. There he stops, and wanders back.

wave of revolutions throughout Spanish America to end Spanish colonialism, were moved to fight

in the United States to end slavery and to make sure that all men and women in this entire hemisphere could be free. Feeding these soldiers was not the hospital's foremost priority in a time of scarcity.

Private Vigil's family originated in Valladolid, Spain and emigrated to Havana, Cuba. Prosperous by mid-19th century standards, he wanted to continue his education in New York. As an idealistic young man, he was also moved by the arguments of the abolitionists. This is how he arrived in Brooklyn and volunteered to fight for the Union against the Confederacy.

The spirit of Augustín Vigil appears walking across the Brooklyn Bridge from Manhattan. He makes his way to Hicks Street, until he reaches Grace Court. There he stops, and wanders back. He is dressed in his Civil War uniform, meanders slowly, stopping to gasp for air. He bends over, resting his hands on his knees as he breathes.

"I have not been fed other than consommé for nine days," he says. "I am hungry."

The spirit then makes a startling claim: He walked from Washington, D.C. to Brooklyn in search of food. "I need sustenance," he says. "I summon food I long for."

He is said to pace through Brooklyn Heights, stand on the corner of Hicks Street and Grace Court, and walk back to the Brooklyn Bridge. He begins to cross the bridge, but then abruptly turns around. The spirit does not recognize the skyline of lower Manhattan any longer and, confused, turns around to return to Grace Court.

"I summon sustenance!" he says.

During the Civil War, Private Vigil was known to have the gift of Dream-Telepathy. This is the ability to communicate with another person while dreaming. Dream-Telepathy would not be validated as an area of scientific inquiry until almost a century later in the 1940s.

The spirit of Private Vigil, however, now makes the audacious claim that, in search of sustenance, he engages in Dream-Telepathy to summon Latin American immigrants to Brooklyn to bring him nourishment.

Private Vigil, wearing a uniform like this Union Army soldier, died in 1861.

He longs for fresh cheese. He desires authentic chocolate. He craves robust distilled spirits, like mescal. The ghost claims that his

Dream-Telepathy is reaching out across the continent. The ghost attributes the abundance of authentic foods from Latin America available in Brooklyn as an answer to his Dream-Telepathy.

"I need sustenance," he tells clairvoyants that have made contact with him. "I need sustenance from my peoples."

Can this be true? Can a ghost engage in Dream-Telepathy? Can the spirit of Augustín Vigil be summoning Latin Americans to emigrate to Brooklyn to provide authentic foods to satisfy the hunger of long-dead Civil War soldiers from the Hispanic world?

It is said that it is too late for Private Vigil. No amount of food will satisfy his hunger. Having passed from this life, he is destined to wander from the Brooklyn Bridge, down Hicks Street to Grace Court, and back again forevermore in hunger.

What of those of us who are living?

Do we owe this cornucopia of abundance to the supplications of a Civil War spirit crying out across the distances of time and geography? Are Latin Americans emboldened to move to Brooklyn with their artisanal foods and liquors as a result of his Dream-Telepathy?

Who can say?

It's a question well worth pondering over a good meal.

The Soul of the Man Who Died of Spontaneous Human Combustion

In the death of Mr. Charles Lewis, what can be said is that his case conforms to spontaneous human combustion.

I t happened on the corner of Cranberry and Willow Streets.

There were witnesses who saw the curious case of Mr. Charles Lewis who burst into flames in one of the more spectacular cases of spontaneous human combustion in the history of Brooklyn.

Yes, there are doubters. Yes, there are the missing entries in the police blotter. Yes, the physical evidence was almost non-existent.

This much is certain, however: on a hot day in July 1875 the extraordinary case of spontaneous human combustion shook Brooklyn Heights. The inexplicable death of Mr. Charles Lewis, who was consumed by flames, still resonates in the imagination of local residents.

There are today, as there were back then when this occurrence unfolded, unbelieving souls who question the witness accounts of the events of that afternoon when Mr. Charles Lewis simply burst into flames. There are those who doubt

On this corner, Mr. Charles Lewis was consumed by flames in a horrific spectacle that scandalized Brooklyn Heights!

the clairvoyants who have communicated with him as he wanders the streets near this intersection, dazed and confused. There are those who imagine other, reasonable and rational, explanations for what occurred.

Perhaps it did occur. Perhaps it did not occur.

It is true that in *Bleak House* Charles Dickens writes of several instances of spontaneous human combustion as a scientific fact. The description of spontaneous human combustion in literature, however, is meager compared to the police and scientific inquiries into the phenomenon. Most cases of spontaneous human combustion, for instance, note that the bodies of the victims are charred, but the extremities seldom display evidence of having been burned. There is little evidence of a fire in the immediate surroundings. Most furniture, walls and floors are described as remaining intact. Police reports often note that greasy marks surround the victim, which is believed to be the remains of human fat.

In the death of Mr. Charles Lewis, what can be said is that his case conforms to spontaneous human combustion as described in the authoritative book, *De Incendiis Corporis Humani Spontaneis*, written by Jonas Dupont in 1763.

In simplest terms, spontaneous human combustion occurs when a person bursts into flames. It is believed to occur as a result of a chemical reaction within the body itself. No external heat source to act as a cause of ignition is cited.

Mr. Charles Lewis has communicated that he himself was astounded that this is how his life ended. Mr. Charles Lewis further claims that there was nothing in his medical history to suggest the accumulation of flammable gases in his torso, or that his was a constitution susceptible to being ignited. Mr. Charles Lewis finally claims there was no solvent or accelerating agent on his person when he burst into flames.

What is, in fact, peculiar about the Ghost of the Man Who Died of Spontaneous Human Combustion is that people who perish this way seldom linger in this world. It is as if their souls are effortlessly propelled to the world beyond. That is not the case with this haunting. Mr. Charles Lewis remains confined to the area of Brooklyn Heights, not venturing east of Henry Street or west of the Promenade that faces the East River. He notes he never crosses north of Old Fulton Street, or ventures below State Street.

This is a rather confined space to limit one's self for all eternity.

Mr. Charles Lewis agrees, and he hopes that enough prayers will be said for his eternal rest that he will be able to move completely to the other side. For now, this man in full, who wanders slowly in dated attire, on occasion enveloped in a mist resembling fumes, is the Ghost of the Man Who Died of Spontaneous Human Combustion.

Don't be afraid: he doesn't smell of sulfur.

Don't be shy: he is courteous.

Don't turn away: he has few friends.

But do do something to help release him from his predicament: say a prayer for the eternal rest of the soul of Mr. Charles Lewis who lingers among the living as the Ghost of the Man Who Died of Spontaneous Human Combustion while on an evening stroll in July 1875 in Brooklyn Heights.

On the corner of Cranberry and Willow Streets in Brooklyn Heights, Mr. Charles Lewis died of spontaneous human combustion in July 1875. There is a fire alarm at that intersection.

The Dutch Ghost of the Tulips

This ghost has a name. It is Willem Kieft. He was born in 1597 and he died in 1647. He was born in Amsterdam and in adulthood was a merchant—and the director of New Netherland. Yes, New Netherland, the European colony that, centuries later, would become New York City.

Before New York was English, it was Dutch. During this era, for two years, 1643-1645, Willem Kieft waged war against the Lenape people, the indigenous inhabitants of the region. It was a savage campaign. This is how David de Vries described one incident

This odd figure, dressed in a coat and hat from the 17th century, searches for green spaces in which to plant bulbs.

in which 120 people were slaughtered:

Infants were torn from their mother's breasts, and hacked to pieces in the presence of their parents, and pieces thrown into the fire and in the water, and other sucklings, being bound to small boards, were cut, stuck, and pierced, and miserably massacred in a manner to move a heart of stone. Some were thrown into the river, and when the fathers and mothers endeavored to save them, the soldiers would not let them come on land but made both parents and children drown.

De Vries wrote this in his journal, *Vertoogh van Nieu Nederland*, subsequently published in 1649 and 1650. It was translated into English by Henry Cruise Murhy centuries later.

Not everyone was pleased with Willem Kieft's "pacification" tactics. He was fired from the Dutch West India Company and he was ordered to answer for his actions before authorities in Amsterdam. He set sail back to Amsterdam to defend himself.

The ghost of Willem Kieft, who died in 1647, is believed to plant tulips throughout Brooklyn to remind the living that Brooklyn was once Dutch.

He would not reach his destination: he died at sea when the *Princess Amelia* sank off the coast of Swansea, Wales on September 27, 1647.

His ghost, however, returned to his beloved New Netherland, fearing that should he continue to Amsterdam he would be found guilty. The ghost of Willem Kieft has nowhere else to go. Consider that he was turned away by Saint Peter and his appeal to the Fallen Angel Lucifer has not been answered. In the centuries that have followed, the ghost claims to be astounded to see the emergence of Grave's End (Gravesend), the most Dutch area of Breuckelen (the Dutch name for the area which is now more commonly known as Brooklyn), grow and become a metropolis.

Grave's End was, in fact, the first Dutch colony on Long Island. Breuckelen was the name for greater Grave's End area. The Dutch Ghost of Brooklyn struggles to communicate: he is not fluent in English despite 365 years of wandering the streets of Brooklyn. He doesn't understand why English has displaced Dutch as the language spoken in Breuckelen. For him, however, English as a second language is the least of his worries, or so he explains to clairvoyants who reach him.

What's foremost on his mind?

That's easy: How to amend for the sins of an unjust war.

The Dutch Ghost of Brooklyn claims to have found a novel way to atone for his sins.

Yes, the ghost of Willem Kieft plants tulips throughout Brooklyn.

He rises at dusk each evening and wanders the parks, planting bulbs. He wants to beautify the borough

The City of Brooklyn — 1879
CURRIER & IVES

and bring pleasure to its residents. He wants to remind the people who live in Brooklyn—an atrocious misspelling of Breuckelen he says time and again—that this remains New Netherland first and foremost.

That's all he ever wanted, he says. That's all he ever hoped to achieve, he argues. That was the only rationale for the military tactics he employed. He wanted to protect and safeguard the colonists. The Dutch Ghost of Brooklyn laments Saint Peter is unmoved. The Dutch Ghost of Brooklyn regrets the Fallen Angel Lucifer is indifferent.

Do you believe him?

Do you believe the Slayer of Children? Do you believe this Savage Warrior against the Defenseless? Do you believe the man who was charged with Carnage against God?

Who can say?

What can be said with confidence, however, is that there are millions of tulips throughout Brooklyn. Who can deny their beauty? What would Brooklyn be without its Dutch tulips?

And this floral beauty is the work of a tireless Dutch ghost who waged war against the innocent and slaughtered infants. Now, this odd figure, dressed in a coat and hat from the 17th century, pacing down the Promenade, searches for green spaces in which to plant bulbs.

This is Dutch, not English, each tulip affirms in its beauty. "So many tulips to plant," he says softly in Dutch. "This work is without end."

Redemption to amend for Carnage against God is always difficult.

If you see his diminutive outline at night, as you sit on a bench along the Brooklyn Promenade, you now know he is only planting tulips. He is only reclaiming Brooklyn for the Dutch, one tulip at a time.

The afterlife is as full of paradoxes as is life itself, isn't it?

The Spirit of the foot fetishist

I magine being a person of wealth who is held in high esteem by your contemporaries. Imagine residing in a fantastic mansion with sweeping views of Lower Manhattan. Imagine being a solid member of society in good standing.

Imagine all of this. Now imagine harboring a sexual fetish that consumed your thoughts.

If you find yourself standing before the Alexander M. White House located at 2 Pierrepont Place in Brooklyn Heights, you might also find yourself feeling the presence of a spirit.

What can be said of the spirit of Alfred T. White whose sexual exuberance can still be felt today?

It is not, however, the spirit of Alexander M. White, the man who built this mansion that you sense. It is the spirit of his son, Alfred T. White.

Alfred T. White was born in 1846 and died in 1921. He is remembered as a great philanthropist who fought for housing reform throughout the city and championed the general betterment of Brooklyn. He was, for four decades, a deacon of the First Unitarian Church of Brooklyn.

His family's fortune was made in importing and exporting, and he continued the tradition.

Not unlike men of privilege during his time, Alfred T. White harbored certain sexual desires few wives were prepared to indulge. It was not that these desires were aberrant or odd, but simply that they were not conducive to procreation. The understanding at that time was that any sexual activity between spouses that did not directly contribute to procreation was superfluous—and to be ignored.

That is, of course, for most people. For a man of standing

It is said the spirit of Alfred T. White, who was a foot fetishist and spent countless hours caressing, kissing and sucking his mistress's toes, is present at this fantastic mansion his father built.

and wealth, on the other hand, social constraints in the arena of human sexuality did not represent an impediment worthy of consideration.

Legend has it that Alfred T. White, in essence, was free to pursue the sexual delights he derived from kissing women's feet, sucking their toes, and watching them pleasure themselves while he caressed their calves. Legend has it that in one of the rooms of the house located at 2 Pierrepont Place, he set up a gynecological table for his mistress. Legend has it that they would spend countless hours indulging his desire.

She would lie back, legs spread, as she pleasured herself. He would sit between her legs, and slowly remove her shoes, gently caressing, kissing and licking each toe. He would place each foot in the stirrups. He would undress as well and masturbate as he fondled her feet, kissed her ankles, and sucked on her toes. She would writhe in pleasure, as she fingered herself and brought herself to orgasm. Theirs was a love affair of carnal desire fulfilled and fantasies pursued. Is it any wonder Alfred T. White was a philanthropist?

This is a haunting of pleasure that reverberates across time.

Do you feel the joy? Do you sense the pleasure? Do you recognize the sexual ecstasy that surrounds this place?

What can be said of a building that contains within it the beauty of life-affirming human sexuality made manifest night after night despite what society may or may not say about such desires?

What can be said of the spirit of Alfred T. White whose sexual exuberance can still be felt today?

There might as well be a playground at Pierrepont!

And there it is!

Good for him! Good for you!

The Soul from September 11

There are those who see him as they look upon the night with believing eyes. There are those who shiver when they see this apparition in the morning light. There are those who say his presence is like a halo. Others claim that it is iridescent—a fine powder suspended in the air.

What all agree, whether they see him in a star-filled night, or in the afternoon sun floating among the trees, is that he is there and he is resplendent.

The location is where Pierrepont Place, Pierrepont Street and Columbia Heights converge.

"And I love you," he says, this soul from September 11 who drifted here, pushed along the southeasterly breezes that prevailed in the morning of September 11, 2001. "Look upon me with believing eyes and I will sing a song for you!"

It has taken three clairvoyants to determine his identity, but it has been done: Victor Martínez Pastrana.

The difficulties in contacting him are ascribed to the muddled nature of his messages. A whirlwind of words were heard by clairvoyants, as if pieces of a puzzle. *And I love you; Windows on the World; Rosario Arrazola; Local 100 of the Hotel Employees and Restaurant Employees Union; I will sing a song for you; Puebla; Asociación Tepeyac de New York; Robin Hood Foundation;* and *Viva la Virgen de Guadalupe.*

Only in this muddle of words was there agreement on this one

It has taken three clairvoyants to determine his identity, but it has been done.

phrase: "Soy Victor Martínez Pastrana."

I am Victor Martínez Pastrana.

In the late morning of September 11 a fine dust—the pulverized remains of incinerated concrete, glass,

It is believed the soul of Victor Martínez Pastrana, who died when the North Tower collapsed, lingers over Brooklyn Heights.

electronics, office furniture, people—began to settle over Brooklyn Heights, carried by the winds across the East River. It was possible to see the fine ash, glistening like shimmering silicone glitter, coating the cars, trees and gardens of Brooklyn Heights. It was then that a suspended, iridescent presence hovered just above the trees at

the intersection of Columbia Heights and Pierrepont Street. In the intervening years, this presence has drifted towards Pierrepont Place.

There are those who recognize the soul of the September 11 victim, which remains in a sort of Purgatory over Brooklyn Heights, for what it is: his illegal presence in this country at the time of his death is now mirrored by the limbo between this world and the next to which he is confined.

What clairvoyants who have communicated with him find remarkable is his magnanimity towards his fate. He feels love and grace, despite the way his own family has been treated, and the disparaging contempt for the value of his life bureaucrats capriciously determined after he perished when the north tower collapsed at 10:28 a.m. on September 11, 2001. He was held in disdain because of his immigration status at the moment of his martyrdom.

He is there, however, suspended over this alien landscape, far from the place of his birth, unable to leave his bonds to New York, unable to touch the face of God.

Look upon him with believing eyes.

He will sing a song for you.

I will sing a song for you, simply because I love you.

The House of the Sibling Suicides

She's in one corner. He's in another corner. Across the ages they remain invisible, but they are both present. This is the House of the Sibling Suicides located at 144 Montague.

Their ghosts are believed to haunt this building, now used primarily for commercial purposes. Back in the 1890s, however, this was the residence of the Coop family. They were well-established and distinguished residents of Brooklyn Heights.

These merits, however, did not afford the family immunity from scandal and tragedy. On the afternoon of February 5, 1893 something terrible happened. Police records document that the authorities were summoned when the half-

Two suicides in the same household in less than a decade stunned the residents of Brooklyn Heights.

naked body of Sallie Coop was found in her third floor bedroom. A pistol lay by her side. Her twin sister, Elizabeth, had married the week before.

It is said that Sallie was distraught at her being separated from Elizabeth for the first time in her life. It is speculated that Elizabeth had falsely promised that she and her husband—the dashing Mr. George Perry Fisk—would move into the Coop family residence. Marriage would not be reason for the twins to be separated by more than a flight of stairs.

This was not the case,

however. The young couple had settled on establishing their own residence. When she learned this, Sallie Coop was overcome and became hysterical. Sallie collapsed and had to be revived with smelling salts. (Elizabeth, it should be pointed out, was also distraught over the looming separation from her twin sister.) But there was nothing to be done. George Perry Fisk was adamant that they would never live at 144 Montague.

Why? Because of secrets revealed. In the course of their courtship Elizabeth had confessed that she and her sister were followers of the Cult of the Menses. This was the widespread belief that repudiated the centuries-old notion that women were "unclean" by virtue of menstruation. The sisters

The ghosts of Sallie Coop and her brother Herman Coop, each of whom committed suicide, are believed to haunt their former home at 144 Montague, known as the House of the Sibling Suicides.

believed that, to the contrary, menstrual blood was life-affirming and that it was a vital link to the Goddess Within.

The sisters, whose menstrual cycles were in sync with each other's, would smear blood on each other's bodies and then wash themselves with wine. They would lick the blood and wine off each other's breasts and torsos. George Perry Fisk was horrified. He vowed that his love for Elizabeth would allow her to transcend this unsound fascination with the morbid and distasteful distraction.

Elizabeth, not unlike Sallie, found nothing aberrant about their beliefs, however. Sallie herself had pointed out to her future brother-in-law that none other than Edgar Allan Poe had written a story where menstrual blood was presented as a metaphor for death. "If you were to read *The Masque of the Red Death* carefully," Sallie explained to him, "you will see how we must transcend the irrational fear of women's bodies and menstrual blood!"

First published in *Graham's Magazine* in May 1842, *The Masque of the Red Death*, a gothic tale, is not as much about the inevitability of death as it is about the deadly fear of menstruation. This was the popular interpretation among the women who adhered to the beliefs of the Cult of the Menses after the Civil War.

This is the passage from *The Masque of the Red Death* cited by followers of the Cult of the Menses for their belief:

In an assembly of phantasms such as I have painted, it may well be supposed that no ordinary appearance could have excited such sensation. In truth the masquerade license of the night was nearly unlimited; but the figure in question had out-Heroded Herod, and gone beyond the bounds of even the prince's indefinite decorum. There are chords in the hearts of the most reckless which cannot be touched without emotion. Even with the utterly lost, to whom life and death are equally jests, there are matters of which no jest can be made. The whole company, indeed, seemed now deeply to feel that in the costume and bearing of the stranger neither wit nor propriety existed. The figure was tall and gaunt, and shrouded from head to foot in the habiliments of the grave. The mask which concealed the visage was made so nearly to resemble the countenance of a stiffened corpse that the closest scrutiny must have had difficulty in detecting the cheat. And yet all this might have been endured, if not approved, by the mad revelers around. But the mummer had gone so far as to assume the type of the Red Death. His vesture was dabbled in blood—and his broad brow, with all the features of the face, was besprinkled with the scarlet horror.

Enlightened women of that age believed *The Mask of the Red Death* was, in fact, a metaphor for menstruation and that this passage reflected men's irrational fear of women's bodies. To complicate matters, unlike most men, George Perry Fisk found nothing arousing in the idea of his wife and her twin sister in a bathtub together, washing each other's blood from their bodies with red wine, savoring the mixture of wine and blood. Unlike most men, George Perry Fisk would have nothing to do with the erotic promise of a *ménage a trois* with twin sisters. Not unlike most proper Victorians, he did not agree with Sallie Coop's interpretation of Edgar Allan Poe's writings.

George Perry Fisk believed his sister-in-law was unhinged and he wanted Elizabeth to establish a distance from her. He wanted to remove her from what he believed to be unhealthy pursuits that bordered on adoration of the gothic.

Nevertheless, no one was prepared for Sallie Coop's decision to take her own life. No one anticipated such a turn of events. The Coop family was shattered over Sallie's suicide. George Perry Fisk found no joy in proof positive that his sister-in-law was emotionally unstable.

Elizabeth would mourn the death of her sister for the rest of her life. Their other sibling, a brother, Herman, who had long championed women's equality—and had encouraged his sisters' worship of menstrual blood—was unable to come to terms with his grief. In 1900 he committed suicide as well.

Two suicides in the same household in less than a decade stunned the residents of Brooklyn Heights. What scandal! What madness! The Coop family residence became known as the House of the Sibling Suicides.

Soon after this second suicide, reports surfaced of ghosts in this building. She's in one corner. He's in another corner. Sallie Coop is seen rubbing menstrual blood on her cheeks and forehead. Herman Coop is seen

carrying a jug of wine, dipping his fingers in it and licking them.

Is it wine? Or is it wine laced with menstrual blood? Do the Ghosts of the Sibling Suicides remain faithful followers of the Cult of the Menses?

Do you see their outlines as you stare upon 144 Montague?

Is it a ghoulish sight?

Or is it a bold affirmation that speaks of the emancipation of womankind?

The Ghosts of Innocents Consumed by Fire

There is no greater haunting in Brooklyn than the vortex of ghosts over the lawns on the eastern stretch of Cadman Plaza.

This is where the Brooklyn Theater once stood, dominating an entire city block along Washington (today Cadman Plaza East) and Johnson Streets. There are those who claim to see a vortex of ghosts swirling in a whirlwind of grief and agony. There are those who feel an inexplicable sense of anxiety in this open space where few Brooklyn residents venture. There are those who report hearing the screams and cries of men, women and children as they are consumed by flames.

It cannot be denied that this spot is the most tragic piece of real estate in the entire borough of Brooklyn. There is reason for this, of course. It is here that the Great Brooklyn Theater Fire of 1876 occurred.

What? You're not familiar with this tragedy?

This would stand as the greatest loss of human life in the city of New York until September 11, 2001. (It is true that the *General Slocum*, a twin-

The Great Brooklyn Theater Fire is believed to have resulted in the death of 278 individuals.

paddlewheel steamboat that caught fire and sank on June 15, 1904 took 1,021 lives, but this was a maritime disaster in the East River, not on land.) The

This is where the Brooklyn Theater once stood, along Washington and Johnson Streets.

Great Brooklyn Theater Fire is believed to have resulted in the death of 278 individuals the night of the fire. Some reports indicate the final death toll was 343 when those who suffered burns and other injuries that night died in the days, weeks and months after the conflagration.

It was described as an inferno, one in which hundreds of people who had come to see the actress Kate Claxton starring in a production of "The Two

Orphans," on the crisp evening of December 5, 1876, would perish. This how the *Brooklyn Union* newspaper, in an article titled "Brooklyn Theater Fire" published on December 6, 1876, described the scene the following day:

The young and the weak were knocked down and trampled upon, and at the doors the people were literally wedged together. One who escaped says that in spite of himself he was carried along, and that the way was made over the bodies of those who had been cast down. Many of these must have been suffocated and become insensible. While these scenes were transpiring the flames had seized upon the house or auditorium, and the dense smoke and intense heat was doing its work in rendering insensible many others. Many losing their senses, becoming frantic, and insane through fear, and utterly despairing of life, leaped into the raging flames beneath. It is impossible at present writing to estimate the loss that occurred in the gallery.

Since that night ghosts haunt this place. Consider that three years after the fire the Harvely's Theater was built on the same site, but was demolished in 1890. The reason? The replacement theater was a commercial failure because theater-goers reported seeing ghosts everywhere.

An office building was then built, and it housed the *Brooklyn Daily Eagle* newspaper. In the busy life of a newspaper during the first half of the 20th century, there was too much commotion for individuals to be distressed by the presence of ghosts around them. The ghosts were innocuous and their voices were lost in the hustle and bustle of typewriters and telephones.

Throughout the decades, however, feelings of unease—and the presence of the anguished souls of those who perished—continued to haunt the living who ventured to this area. There were too many painful memories. There were so many ghosts trapped in a vortex of anguish. Here, for your examination, is one of the accounts published to commemorate the event, which kept memory of the Great Brooklyn Theater Fire alive in the public's mind. In an interview published in the *New York Times* on November 30, 1885, the actress Kate Claxton recalls:

We thought we were acting for the best in continuing the play as we did, with the hope that the fire would be put out without difficulty, or that the audience would leave gradually or quietly. But the result proved that it was not the right course… The curtain should have been kept down until the flames had been extinguished, or if it had been found impossible to cope with them, the audience should have been calmly informed that indisposition on the part of some member of the company, or some unfortunate occurrence behind the scenery compelled a suspension of the performance, and they should have been requested to disperse as quietly as they could. Raising the curtain created a draft which fanned the flames into fury.

The public's anguish and anxiety continued.

The vortex of ghosts was described as a funnel of suffering souls in a kind of Purgatory. There was a consistent stream of ghost sightings, paranormal activity and a sense of anxiety among the living. It reached such a level of despair that city officials decided to raze the entire block, part of the urban renewal scheme for downtown Brooklyn that included the creation of Cadman Plaza, an urban park, which resembles the vast lawn of a cemetery.

The serenity of this place—the approximate location of the theater is a bit north of where the New York Supreme Court Building now stands—offers a refuge for the ghosts. Despite the creation of a tree-covered park, however, there are still reports of a swirling funnel-shaped whirlwind of souls of the victims.

> Do you sense their presence as you walk among the tree-covered lawns of Cadman Plaza? Do you suffer the horror these victims felt as they were engulfed by flames and smoke? Can you feel their fear and panic, their screams and supplications to Saint Catherine of Siena as these innocents were consumed by fire?
>
> Can you see the Ghosts of the Great Brooklyn Theater Fire of 1876 surrounding you in a whirlwind of agony?

Clairvoyants who wander through the park report that scores of ghosts recite desperate prayers to Saint Catherine of Siena, a 14th century saint who is the patron saint of those who fear fire and of firefighters.

This is not surprising. In 19th century Brooklyn many structures were made of wood and the rapidly-expanding industrial economy resulted in frequent fires and factory explosions. In consequence, the Cult of Saint Catherine of Siena emerged as one of the more popular devotionals throughout Brooklyn. Catholics dedicated masses to her seeking protection against fires. The Brooklyn Cult of Saint Catherine of Siena had tens of thousands of devotees.

In the years following the fire there were reports of seven apparitions of Saint Catherine of Siena where the theater once stood. Throughout the 20th century other witnesses have reported seeing her in the Cadman Plaza area hovering above the trees. And in one of the more startling claims, in the confusion of September 11, 2001, witnesses reported seeing her, looking towards the Brooklyn Bridge and the World Trade Center, screaming, tears running down her face as the Twin Towers burned and collapsed onto hundreds of firefighters.

This is the only known instance of a saint screaming in horror.

Some claim that the number of firefighters killed that day—343—is the exact number of actual victims of the Great Brooklyn Theater Fire of 1876. Some clairvoyants claim that this was price exacted to release the souls of those who died at this spot in 1876. Others believe her screams prevented additional deaths by fire that day.

It is an odd claim, but one that speaks of the power of the vortex of ghosts that haunt the environs where the Great Brooklyn Theater Fire of 1876 took place. (If you are curious, there is an obelisk memorial to these victims not far from the main entrance at 5th Avenue and 25th Street at Green-Wood Cemetery. There are 103 victims buried in a common grave.) The souls of these dead are believed to remain at Cadman Plaza, however, where they lost their lives.

✠ Dumbo ✠

The Ghost of the Bewildered Belgian Woman

S he was an immigrant from Belgium. That much is certain. She worked for the Fulton Ferry Company when Robert Fulton began a ferry service that linked the City of New York on Manhattan Island to the Village of Brooklyn on Long Island. The year was 1814. The location was Fulton Landing, which today is known as DUMBO.

Belgians in Brooklyn were not uncommon. Many Belgian immigrants to New York settled in Wallabout Bay, that small body of water where DUMBO and Williamsburg collide. They began to arrive in the 1630s. These French-speaking Walloon immigrants were primarily Catholic.

History records her name as Justine Delvaux, but not much else is known about her. Her ghost is often seen along Main Street, between Front and Plymouth Streets. She is believed to be in her early 20s. She is believed to have been a dazzling beauty. She was often approached by men attracted to her radiant eyes and captivating smile.

Legend has it her beauty proved to be her undoing. Legend tells of the hearts she broke when she fended off the advances of many suitors.

Her parents were strict, and they refused to let her

Saint Gertrude of Nivelles, the Patron Saint of those who fear mice and rats, could not save Justine Delvaux.

contemplate indulging any serious contact with men who were not Walloons. The heart, however, seldom follows the dictates of reason.

She laughed at jokes Protestant passengers told her as they waited for the ferry to arrive. She blushed when young Jewish men complimented her on her beauty. She found the Irish to be charmers, and the Spaniards to be delightful.

Women were jealous of her, often associating

her effortless sociability with loose morals. Nothing was further from the truth.

The ghost of Justine Delvaux claims she was a proper young woman in life, and only engaged men in conversation by way of performing her duties as an employee of the Fulton Ferry Company.

There is no evidence to contradict her. But it is conceivable that she inspired jealousy among the women who looked down on the French-speaking Belgian Catholics.

It is said that it became well-known that Justine Delvaux feared rats. It is well-known that she availed herself to Saint Gertrude of Nivelles, the patron saint of those who fear mice and rats. (Yes, there is a patron saint for those who fear rodents.) It is well-known that she was mocked for her fear of these small mammals. Many gentlemen teased her by bringing rats, both living and dead, with them onto the ferry. It is said that Robert Fulton was not amused by any of this, fearing that a rat infestation would tarnish the reputation of the ferry service he had established.

Legend has it there came a time when two sisters, enraged at the lavish attention paid her by their brothers, conspired to cast a spell upon the Fulton Landing. These sisters invoked an infestation of rats to rise from the East River.

It is said that these rats, demonic and possessed, conjured through Wiccan spells,

numbering in the millions, were powerful enough to cover the streets surrounding Fulton Landing. These rats swarmed

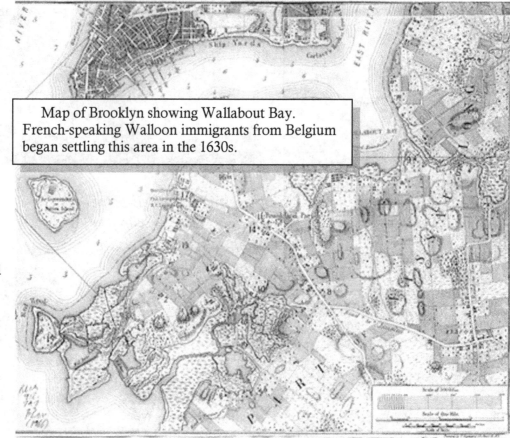

Map of Brooklyn showing Wallabout Bay. French-speaking Walloon immigrants from Belgium began settling this area in the 1630s.

from all directions. They seized Justine Delvaux, knocking her down, engulfing her body.

This assault and abduction occurred after the last ferry had concluded its late-night service across the East River. Her screams went unheard. Her pleas to Saint Gertrude of Nivelles were drowned out by the swarms of rats that covered her body. Her desperation was unseen by mortal men.

The army of rats dragged her, as she writhed and struggled in vain against these creatures. Her nails scratched the cobblestones in front powerHouse Books and One Girl Cookies.

Legend has it that after these rats seized her and dragged her away, they descended into the underworld of New York City. There they would remain until the New York City subway was constructed. It is here under the

streets of DUMBO that the New York City subway rats originated.

Were the muffled pleas—

which went unanswered by Saint Gertrude of Nivelles—of the desperate Belgian immigrant Justine Delvaux that gave rise to the army of rats that inhabit New York's underground?

Can you hear it? What does it sound like?

What do you imagine when you hear the desperate, muffled cries of a young woman seized along the abandoned streets of Brooklyn's waterfront late at night as she was dragged to her death by a hoard of possessed rats?

It is horror!

Can you hear them? Can you hear the multitudes of rats rising from their dormant existence as they move through New York's subway tunnels?

It is the horror that one feels when gazing upon the army of rats that possess the New York City subway.

The Ghost of the Lost Girl

She claims her name is Patricia, which was a popular name for girls in the 1940s in Brooklyn. She claims she is 11 years old. She claims she is lost and all she wants is to return home, but she doesn't know how to make her way back. She is just trying to find her way home.

It is the ghost of a lost girl that wanders the streets of DUMBO. One psychic has traced her clockwise travels from

She doesn't want to get home late because she doesn't want to miss the "I Love Lucy" television program.

There are witness reports of the ghost of a young girl in the area since the mid-1950s. She is described as wearing a long white dress, almost like a dressing gown. She has long brown hair and wears slippers, as if she were about to take a dance

Lucy" television program. The only other thing she explains to the psyhics who have made contact with her is that she has "willed" flower shops to the area. She enjoys the smell of roses. She also loves chocolate. This is why she "willed" chocolatiers here, Jacques Torres first, and now Conrad Miller. She wants to enjoy the smell of chocolates. And she also longs for pumpkin Whoopie Pies and macaroons.

She claims to have "willed" bakeries that offer these pastries as well.

There is not much else she says, other than express her frustration at not being able to find her way home.

Have you seen this innocent child? Have you seen the apparition of this lost girl wandering the cobblestone streets in this area of DUMBO?

The ghost of the lost girl claims to spend her nights under the Manhattan Bridge Archway Plaza.

Pearl to York Streets, then she turns towards Adams Street. From there, she heads towards the river until reaching John Street, and turns onto Pearl Street once more. She claims to rest at Anchorage Place and Water Street when weary. When the weather is inclement, she takes refuge inside the Manhattan Bridge Archway Plaza.

lesson.

There was always speculation that this young girl was a victim of violent thugs of one of the working-class gangs, the ones that were photographed by Bruce Davidson in the 1950s in various sections of Brooklyn. If she was, she isn't saying.

She does say she doesn't want to get home late because she doesn't want to miss the "I Love

Have you sensed her disorientation as she hesitates in her measured steps?

Is it true that there are those who leave flowers, chocolates and pasteries for her on one of the picnic tables along the Manhattan Bridge Archway Plaza?

Have you tried to help her make her way home?

The Ghosts of the Lynched Mexicans

From a distance late at night when it's foggy it's possible to see the outlines of two men whose lifeless bodies sway slowly near the Manhattan Bridge underpass off Front Street.

When the subway trains cross the bridge the men are said to shake like rag dolls. They are not dolls, however. They are the corpses of two innocents who were lynched by an angry mob in 1852 after they arrived in New York seeking clarification on the meaning of the Land Act of 1851.

To understand the Land Act of 1851 it is first necessary to refer back to the Treaty of Guadalupe-Hidalgo of 1848.

They ran to a series of buildings near Front and Pearl Streets. There they were surrounded and seized upon by the mob...

And of course this all makes more sense if one remembers that between the Treaty of Guadalupe-Hidalgo of 1848 and the Land Act of 1851 there was the discovery of gold at Sutter's Mill in California in 1849.

It is also necessary to remember that the United States, like most countries in the world, is unexceptional when it comes to violating its international obligations when these obligations are seen to be inconvenient.

This settled, the tale of the ghosts of the lynched Mexicans is a story that has its origins in the peace treaty that concluded the American invasion of Mexico, euphemistically known as the Mexican-American War. That military engagement ended on February 2, 1848 with the signing of the Treaty of Guadalupe-Hidalgo. Article VII of that treaty states:

Mexicans now established in territories previously belonging to Mexico, and which remain for the future within the limits of the United States, as defined by the present treaty, shall be free to continue where they now reside, or to

The place where the Mexican attorneys were lynched was knocked down when the Manhattan Bridge construction began in 1901.

remove at any time to the Mexican Republic, retaining the property which they possess in the said territories, or disposing thereof, and removing the proceeds wherever they please, without their being subjected, on this account, to any contribution, tax, or charge whatever.

There was opposition in Washington to this Article, simply because as it became well-known that under Mexican law women could own property in their own names, many American legislators believed that this

Discrimination against Mexicans is a long American tradition.

precedent would lead non-Mexican American women—the suffragettes—to agitate for greater rights for women in the United States. Politicians throughout the United States feared that the rights of Mexican women would inflame the passions of hysterical American women.

Indeed, Washington officials feared that if Mexican women in the U.S. were allowed to own property, the natural order of things would

come undone, where the suppression of womankind was concerned.

That fear, however, was quickly overshadowed by a more immediate reality: the discovery of gold in California in 1849 at Sutter's Mill, not far from San Francisco.

Suddenly, the prospect of vast veins of gold running through the newly-acquired territories electrified the rich and powerful in New York and Washington. More germane to our haunting, the United States was not prepared to

entertain the idea that vast stretches of properties containing vast fortunes of gold could belong to Mexicans.

In New York, there was much speculation on what this meant. The story of Ygnacio Martínez was told as a cautionary tale. Ygnacio Martínez was born in Mexico City in 1774, enlisted in the army and was upwardly mobile in life. He served as the fourth mayor of San Francisco

(1837-1838), and was the beneficiary of a land grant in what today is most of Contra Costa County in northern California. When he died in June 1848, his widow, Martina Arellanes de Martínez, inherited all his property.

This vast tract of land—nestled between San Francisco and Sutter's Mill—might hold a fortune in gold, many in New York speculated. American politicians in Washington were not about to entertain the thought that such wealth be controlled by a foreigner, or a woman. Much less a foreign woman!

As such, in a matter of months, Congress passed the Land Act of 1851. This Act established the Public Land Commission whose purpose was to validate—or invalidate—all the property titles held by Mexican citizens now residing in territories acquired from Mexico. Article VII of the Treaty of Guadalupe-Hidalgo was reduced to just another international obligation to be ignored, and violated.

It should come as no surprise that the Public Land Commission, under the authority of the Land Act of 1851, found that Martina Arellanes de Martínez—and scores of thousands of other Mexican nationals—was ineligible to have title to her property validated. And so began the systematic seizure—Communist-style confiscations—of millions of acres of property Mexicans owned throughout the United States.

The ghosts of the lynched Mexicans were attorneys who set sail to New York and were staying at the Spanish Hotel near present-day Wall Street in Manhattan. They had arrived in New York to advocate on behalf of the Mexican nationals who were being disenfranchised by the decisions of the Public Land Commission.

There were very few Mexican families who could defend themselves, or at least attempt to maneuver the system in their favor. (Many Mexicans terrorized by the edicts of the Public Land Commission hastily married their daughters to American citizens, and transferred their properties to the names of their Anglo-American sons-in-law. María Antonia Martínez, daughter of Ygnacio and

speaking Spanish. It was here that word spread that these were Mexicans seeking to reclaim territories out West that were rich in gold. It was rumored that they were in New York to inflame the passions of American women by encouraging them to demand the right to own property. (The realization that the Treaty of Guadalupe-Hidalgo allowed Mexican women the right to own property in their own names caused great excitement among American suffragettes at the Seneca Falls Convention in 1848.) Word spread that

suspended from a second floor railings of the buildings. Those structures were demolished half a century later, a necessary step in the urban accommodation required for the construction of the Manhattan Bridge, which began in 1901.

One clairvoyant who has tried to communicate with the lynched Mexicans reports that one man is named Zavala and the other is named Córdoba. They are otherwise silent. They are helpless. They have been forsaken.

Do you see them? Are you a witness to the injustice they endured at the hands of a Brooklyn mob?

Some claim to see the Virgin of Guadalupe near these lynched apparitions. Others, in contrast, claim to see the two Mexican attorneys at the Gran Eléctrica Mexican restaurant on Front Street. A few witnesses report seeing them at Pedro's on Jay Street.

Lynching, New York City, 1863

Martina Martínez, for instance, married William Richardson, an Englishman who was a naturalized U.S. citizen, and even then, the Martínez family was unable to keep title to certain land holdings.) These attorneys arrived in Brooklyn by ferry, as part of their travel to the greater New York area.

It was here that the men, leaving a private residence near Washington and Front Streets were overheard

they were here to entice witches, lesbians, hysterics and other unnatural radical women with delusions of equality with men. It was here that the men were seized upon by a mob.

The men fled as they realized they were under attack, and, confused among the unfamiliar streets, they ran to a series of buildings near Front and Pearl Streets. There they were surrounded and seized upon by the mob. The men were lynched, their bodies

If you had been seized upon by a mob of Americans and had been lynched, where would you go to soothe your throat, or quench your thirst?

Given America's history of lynching, there may come a time when you might very well have to consider such a question in your own afterlife.

For now, clear your throat, speak up and proceed with caution through the Land of Lynchings!

The Soul of the Falling Jew

It is a haunting as challenging to comprehend as is *The Guide for the Perplexed* written by Maimonides in the 12th century C.E.

What can one say about the Soul of the Falling Jew, seen by some who look at 100 Jay Street in Brooklyn?

What can one say about a man who, in life, was protected by the Angel Nemamiah, who looked upon him as a man of righteousness working for just causes? What can be said about a man held in high esteem by his contemporaries for all his good deeds? What can be said of a man beloved by his family, a family which he loved more than anything in the world?

What can be said when a

He was possessed by thoughts of self-destruction and, in his illness, he made that fateful decision which a minute could no longer reverse.

man is then possessed by the Angel Kezef and is driven to commit an act that is as regrettable as it is irreversible?

In a minute there is time for decisions and revisions which a minute will reverse—not!

For the family and friends, colleagues and admirers of Michael Rothenberg, the man who is seen falling from a height at 100 Jay Street, it is a haunting of unspeakable sadness. His is a destiny that questions the nature of truth and the limits of justice.

It is as Maimonides first

expressed:

My object in adopting this arrangement is that the truths should be at one time apparent and at another time concealed. Thus we shall not be in opposition to the Divine Will (from which it is wrong to deviate) which has withheld from the multitude the truths required for the knowledge of God, according to the words, "The secret of the Lord is with them that fear Him (Psalm 25:14)"

In a more contemporary understanding of this haunting, it is a tragic case informed by the existentialism of Judaism as advocated by Emmanuel Levinas. This is to say, Michael Rothenberg was distracted by the notion of otherness and the melancholy

Building where Michael Rothenberg committed suicide.

of despair. "The Other precisely reveals himself in his alterity not in a shock negating the I, but as the primordial phenomenon of gentleness," Emmanuel Levinas declared, claiming this idea as a defining statement of his philosophy.

"I could have written that sentence," Michael Rothenberg is said to have said.

In the hesitancy for enduring the challenges of life, the melancholy of the ebbs and flows between health and illness, the rational and the irrational, hope and despair, there came an instant when the *grace* of the Angel Nemamiah was momentarily overpowered by the *nihilism* of the Angel Kezef.

He was possessed by thoughts of self-destruction and, in his illness, he made that fateful decision which a minute could no longer reverse.

To his credit, and as evidence of the righteousness with which he lived his life, as the Angel Kezef pushed him down faster towards the Earth, it is the Angel Nemaniah who intervened, rescuing his soul before his body touched the ground.

"Has death killed this nightmare that I've been living?" it is said he asked the Angel Nemaniah.

No one can say with certainly, other than behold with awe the image of the man falling from a height. The only comfort is knowing his soul was saved by the Angel Nemaniah seconds before his heart stopped beating.

One cannot forbid tragedy. One, however, can strive to rise above it.

Michael Rothenberg said so himself.

Cover of The Guide for the Perplexed *written by Maimonides in the 12ᵗʰ Century*

The Ghost of the Semen Donor

It stood near Plymouth and Little Streets, in what is today the Vinegar Hill area of DUMBO. It was a building that housed a Coven of Witches.

Yes, Brooklyn is full of witches and warlocks. Wiccans have long flocked to Brooklyn, with its vast expanses and many enclosed homes that offer privacy for those seeking discretion.

It is here that, in the 1830s and 1840s, a terrifying Coven of Witches assembled. These women were followers of the Cult of Sacred Semen, believing in the magical and life-giving power of sperm.

They consumed semen and also used it as an ointment in their rituals. As their Coven grew, it became necessary to procure greater quantities of semen. This is where the haunting has its origins.

Cronus fathered Zeus (or Jupiter), the god of the gods in Greek (and Roman) mythology. Cronus is therefore the originator of divine life. It was to honor his name that these witches concluded that the only way they could secure a steady supply of semen was to abduct a man whose name bore a resemblance to Cronus. They would find a suitable candidate and they would imprison him in their Coven. This is how two witches combed through the lists of

The witches never spoke to him. He could overhear them speak of their joy that he was giving them "beautiful sons."

The house where the Coven of Witches assembled was in the Vinegar Hill district, near Plymouth and Little Streets.

new immigrants arriving in New York to search for appropriate candidates for their nefarious purposes.

We know this because clairvoyants have made contact with the ghost of a handsome young man who is seen wandering Vinegar Hill near the intersection of Plymouth and Little Streets. He is dressed in the peasant clothing that was common throughout much of northern Europe in the 1830s and 1840s. He is of Germanic descent both clairvoyants agree. There is disagreement on his name, however. One clairvoyant is convinced he says his name is Kronenberg. Another one claims it is Croneberger. A third insists it is Throneburg.

What is not in dispute is the tale he tells: A young man,

with dirty blond hair, deep blue eyes and standing just over six feet, he was of muscular build and newly arrived in New York. He made his way to Brooklyn, where, one evening at a tavern off Water Street, he was approached by two women. At this time, the only women who ventured into drinking establishments were prostitutes. He believed these women were whores plying their trade. He was mistaken. He now believes that he was drugged, or bewitched. Either way, he was abducted or seduced by them. His next memory is waking up, tied to a bed, naked and being "milked."

Several witches were present and participated. They murmured chants. When he reached orgasm, their eyes opened wildly and they were delighted in the copious amount of ejaculate. They gathered as much of it as they could. They rubbed their fingers in it. They held it close to their nostrils. They licked their fingertips. These witches were practitioners of semenatophagy, which is the ritual ingestion of human semen and other sexual fluids.

This ghost, who claims to have been Episcopalian in life, recalls the witches repeating Psalm 110:3 which states: "Thy people shall be willing in the day of thy power, in the beauties of holiness from the womb of the morning: thou hast the dew of thy youth."

The dew of youth: semen.

He believes the witches were impregnating themselves with his semen. He claims he was imprisoned in a small, windowless room, shackled to the wall like a Negro slave. He claims he was "milked" every night. He claims that he was well-fed and well-cared for, the way one covets a prized horse or bull.

The witches never spoke to him. He could overhear them speak of their joy that he was giving them "beautiful sons." (He testifies these witches engaged in female infanticide, drowning the baby girls they birthed.) They wanted only sons. They wanted only male offspring to protect them from the world, ever so hostile to their kind.

The Ghost of the Semen Donor tells of the exhaustion and loneliness of his existence, cut off from sunlight, imprisoned in this place, unable to escape. The Ghost of the Semen Donor tells of the growing demand for his ejaculate, of witches from distant places traveling to this Coven in Brooklyn for his sperm. The Ghost of the Semen Donor tells of arguments heard among the witches, of the bewildering and voracious appetite for his ejaculate, of the growing elaborate ritual associated with his nightly "milking." The Ghost of the Semen Donor recalls the mounting horror and anguish he felt as his enslavement continued without end.

He then recalls that, one night, there was silence. None of the witches entered the room where he was held. This was followed by a day where no one brought him food, or

removed the pots where he performed his daily ablutions. Had he been abandoned? Had the authorities raided this Coven of Witches? Would he die of thirst or hunger?

Then, he heard noises. He smelled food. He heard the sound of drinks being poured. He sensed the incantations and spells these women recited.

The door opened. Three witches entered the room. One removed the pots, while the others gave him drink and food. Afterwards, he was bathed and left to rest. A few hours later, the door opened. He was awakened.

Other witches he had never seen before were present. He was stripped as was the routine, and they began the process of arousing him, a precursor to his ritual "milking." Only this time, there was friction in the air.

Cronus, father of Zeus

The witches were in competition, not harmony, with each other. The unfamiliar witches seemed to dominate the scene.

The moment he reached orgasm, there was a frenzied dash for his ejaculate. Two of the witches licked the semen from his body, while three others fought them off. Another reached for his loins, and began the process of "milking" him again.

The witches bickered among themselves. They continued to "milk" him multiple times throughout the evening and into the night, each subsequent ejaculate less substantial than the one before. One witch stood over him and uttered an incantation, a spell on those who bore his name, he claims.

The ritual continued to the point of exhaustion. He lost consciousness. In their mad desire for his semen, they killed him unintentionally.

The Ghost of the Semen Donor remembers looking down at his own corpse. The witches unshackled him. They carried his body to the canal, and dumped him there. He now wanders the streets at night, disoriented and longing for the mortal life of which he was deprived.

Legend says an incantation was made that night and that to this day, men of Cronus—Kronenbergs and Cronebergers and Throneburgs—are under a spell, freely surrendering their sperm to Brooklyn witches so that these otherwise barren women can bear children.

Can this be true? Can this tale transmitted to clairvoyants by this Teutonic youth of Vinegar Hill be true?

Was he "milked" to death by witches desperate for his semen? Is it true that his sperm was so electrifying that today there is an electric power substation in the very spot where he was imprisoned by these witches?

Is their incantation enduring? Are there bewitched men today under a spell who freely surrender their semen to Brooklyn witches?

Is this what the Ghost of the Semen Donor tells you when your thoughts meet his, along the lonely streets of Vinegar Hill?

The Spirit of the Slave Miranda

*I*t is a testament to devotion to one's duty however one defines duty to be. It is the story of a woman, a black slave named Miranda, who, entrusted with taking care of her mistress, remains intent on doing just that. It is the story of a haunting that continues to baffle waiters, waitresses and restaurateurs throughout Brooklyn to this day.

Here are the facts as generally agreed upon. An elegant black woman enters a restaurant alone. She is dressed in a contemporary, understated manner and asks for a table for one. She will order three or four appetizers and three or four other dishes. She may order a glass of wine to be paired appropriately with an entrée or two as they are served. She samples a bite from all the dishes, but seldom finishes any specific appetizer or entrée. She never asks for dessert, but she will order coffee or tea, depending on the weather. When the bill arrives, she pays cash, leaving a generous tip, usually between 25% and 35% of the bill. She will then leave, never asking that any of the unfinished plates be wrapped up.

It's odd for a woman dining alone to order several appetizers, much less several entrées. It's peculiar for a diner to inquire about how each dish is prepared or ask about specific ingredients.

Most waiters and waitresses assume she is a food critic; or simply a charming, odd character, fastidious in her

An elegant black woman enters a restaurant alone. She is dressed in a contemporary, understated manner and asks for a table for one.

eating habits. On occasion she asks to speak to the chef or manager to ask technical questions about how a certain dish was prepared. She always

Is this a photograph of the slave Miranda, taken in the 1940s?

introduces herself as Miranda.

Then, after she has long left the place, her haunting becomes evident. At the conclusion of the meal service, when the restaurant is closing down for the night, confusion ensues. The cash registers do not include her bill. The meal tickets fail to document her

order. The money isn't missing, but the day's sales do not reflect her presence whatsoever. When waiters and waitresses "double check" their tickets, they find that, sequentially, her specific ticket is blank, as if it had been inadvertently skipped.

There is disagreement over this discrepancy.

How could the sale of this meal service not show up? How could an order ticket be blank? How can the bottle of wine she ordered—from which only a single glass was poured for her alone in the course of the evening—be found to be unopened? How could there be no evidence of this diner's existence, other than the corresponding cash tip left behind for service? Is everyone crazy? Is it a case of mass delusion?

Some suspicious (or savvy) waiters and waitresses claim they believed she was a "mystery diner," but it becomes clear that it is, in fact, just a mystery!

Who is this Miranda? Who is this diner who wasn't there?

And then it becomes clear!

Is the legend real? Can the myth be true? Is this Miranda the black slave owned by Colonel William Axtell, a prominent figure in Brooklyn during the Revolutionary era who remained a staunch loyalist to the British crown? Is

Miranda the slave he ordered to take care of his mistress, Alva, whom, out of jealousy, he kept locked up in a series of apartments in his mansion, known as Melrose Hall?

Is it true that when Colonel William Axtell was ordered to the wilderness of the Ohio Valley to suppress an uprising among Native Americans who resisted the intrusion of English settlers, he absented himself, locking Alva in her apartment, giving Miranda the only key and ordering Miranda to care for her mistress? Is Miranda the slave who died unexpectedly, and in consequence, Alva was left locked away, and starved to death?

It is said that Miranda, unaware that she has died, today wanders Brooklyn, mindful of her duties to feed her mistress. It is said that Miranda is baffled that no cooks are working in the kitchens at Melrose Hall.

That's the reason she frequents eating establishments in search of appropriate places to eat.

It is said she is forever compiling a roster of adequate restaurants in order to make recommendations for her mistress, who must by now be ravenous with hunger.

In the last known photograph taken of her, in the 1940s, Miranda appears demur and elegant, waiting to be seated at a private booth at a steakhouse off Flatbush Avenue near Grand Army Plaza.

One psychic who has made contact with her reports that Miranda explains her last instructions from Colonel William Axtell were to look after her mistress. It is her duty to ensure her meals are to her satisfaction, that her linens are changed, that the accoutrements she required for her daily ablutions are prepared, and that she has

appropriate reading material to occupy her days. Miranda further explains that she compiles a list of appropriate establishments that serve adequate provisions or meals.

Can this be true?

Can Brooklyn boast one other-worldly food critic who wanders the borough in search of exceptional dining experiences?

Is *Zagat* prepared to entertain reviews from the world beyond?

Make of it what you will, gentle reader, but at the end of this book is a list of cafés, gourmet provision shops and restaurants that have been recommended by the spirit of the slave Miranda. She should know where to eat since she has been sampling meals throughout Brooklyn since the Revolutionary War!

Bon appétit!

BROOKLYN EAGLE POST CARD, SERIES 56, No. 335.

FLATBUSH AVENUE. MELROSE PARK ON RIGHT.

19th century photograph of where Melrose Hall once stood off Bedford Avenue.

✠ Park Slope ✠

The Ghost Restorer of BAM Harvey Theater

What is it about this place? What is it about the astounding theatrical performances that take place here? What is it about the place itself? There is something about the layers of paint, the cracked plaster, the exposed brick, the scent of dust. It is as if you have entered a tomb that has only recently been discovered.

There are ghosts here, of course. There are several ghosts. No one doubts that fact. But only one has been contacted by a

There are several ghosts here. No one doubts that fact. But only one has been contacted by a medium.

medium. Yes, only one.

His name is Alfred P. Clark, and he died on June 27, 1889. He was 76 years old at the time, and he had worked as a modeler for the New York Yacht Club. It was, by his own account, a splendid life. It provided him with an adequate livelihood. He was able to provide for all of his

family's material needs.

It also afforded him a front-row seat into the lives of the privileged. His talents were respected and his work was admired. He built model yachts for the elite of his era. Titans of industry. Political leaders. Cultural luminaries of the age.

Mr. Clark smiles from the world beyond at the memory of it. There were times when he would be invited to sail aboard the yachts of the rich and powerful. How else would he be able to construct a model faithful

Interior of the BAM Harvey Theater

to the original, he was asked?

Good question, he replied. He smiled. A date was set. They would sail along the Hudson. Did the wind sweep life into the sails? Did he have the chance to dance under the moonlight? Did he regal life in the light of day? Was he ever swept off his feet by the thrill of sailing?

Oh, yes, Mr. Clark replies. He danced in the light of day on the decks of luxury yachts, and he tasted champagne under the stars of the Milky Way.

All these pleasures unfolded while adrift in the gentle currents of the Hudson River forever dancing and meandering towards

was once alive, and I danced on the decks of yachts that sailed the Hudson River, with a flute of champagne in hand and the gaiety of laughter and merriment around me! I was once alive!"

And now, he notes, he is confined to the darkness of the theater. He is not sure how he ended up here. He is not sure who his other metaphysical companions are who also inhabit the BAM Harvey Theater. They seldom communicate with him.

The only thing that is certain is that, upon dying, he awoke to find himself here. This theater opened in 1904, 15 years after his death. It was the Majestic

abandoned. Those were the lonely years, Mr. Clark says, since the living seldom wandered its halls, other than neighborhood teenagers who used to break in to drink, smoke weed and make out. Not until 1987 when Harvey Lichtenstein was scouting a venue for the Next Wave Festival was this place—and this haunting— rediscovered.

The living argued, Mr. Clark reports. Some wanted to transform the place into a post-modern showplace of glass and metal. A few wanted to create "vertical gardens" as they are inclined to do in distant places

Alfred P. Clark died on June 27, 1889.

the Atlantic. The memory of feeling blood rushing through his veins remains so distant and familiar. The memory of life is so far, but so near. "I keep seeing myself dancing in my memories of life," Mr. Alfred P. Clark says. "Yes, I

Theater back then. The first production was "The Wizard of Oz." It would remain a theater for decades, until it became a movie house in 1942. Decades later, in 1968, it would be

where design is cutting edge, such as Paris, Stockholm and Mexico City. Most, however, were enamored by the water-stained ceilings, the cracked plaster, and the exposed steel evocative of a ruined Greco-Roman amphitheater. It's not hard to see which vision prevailed: this place could be Pompeii.

The ghosts influenced the decision, Mr. Clark reports. The ghosts possessed the minds of the living. The ghosts wanted nothing that would be unfamiliar to the sense of place and time in which they had existed while alive.

There was a price to pay for this: Labor.

How does one restore, and then maintain, what is supposed to be "decrepit" and "ruined"? How does one remain faithful to the sense of abandonment of a structure that is in constant use? How does one become swept off his or her feet while wandering the vaults of a place that is designed to feign a state of perpetual abandonment?

How does one make manifest the beauty of decay? The answer is one word: Urine.

The Ghost Restorer of BAM Harvey Theater, Mr. Alfred P. Clark, deceased in 1889,

confesses that the careful application of urine maintains the theater in a perpetual state of apparent abandonment.

The medium who has made contact with him reports that it is a difficult task.

"This place would reek of a public toilet were it not for dietary measures," the Ghost Restorer of BAM Harvey Theater explains. "We must abstain from coffee; red wine; scotch or bourbon; and

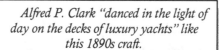

Alfred P. Clark "danced in the light of day on the decks of luxury yachts" like this 1890s craft.

asparagus."

He claims these are substances that would otherwise give an unpleasant scent to the urine applied to the iron columns and exposed brick. What, then, gives the theater its perpetual aroma of musk and dust, of only having recently been uncovered?

The Ghost Restorer of BAM

Harvey Theater then reveals the secret: The essence of celery and condensed milk as transformed into urine.

The ghosts who inhabit this place are on a strict diet of celery and condensed milk to sweeten the taste and smell of their urine. It is only then that it can be used to maintain the BAM Harvey Theater in a perpetual state of apparent disrepair. It is only then that audiences are swept off their feet by the sense of archaeological discovery. It is only then that splendid performances can take place on that stage. It is only then that performers can dance in the light of day and taste champagne under the stars of the Milky Way as Mr. Alfred P. Clark did while alive, while aboard the yachts that sailed the Hudson in the 1860s and 1870s.

It is only then that the audience can keep their spirits dancing, enveloped by the seductive scent of the celery- and condensed milk-infused aromas of the urine of the Ghost Restorer of BAM Harvey Theater.

Do you recognize it? Do you know the scent of celery- and condensed milk-infused urine when you inhale it?

Do you know the secrets of the ghosts who labor for eternity to give the appearance of abandonment?

Or are your thoughts too busy dancing of their own accord, if not under the stars of the Milky Way, then at least under the spell of ghostly urine?

Rise! Dance! Dance in the well of the BAM Harvey Theater, under the spell of Mr. Alfred P. Clark's ethereal urine! It's all around you!

Rise! Dance! Dance in the well of the BAM Harvey Theater as if you were dancing in the light of day on the decks of luxury yachts! Dance as if you were sipping champagne under the stars of the Milky Way! Dance until you feel the blood rushing through your veins! Dance while you are alive!

And look around you!

There is beauty in decay.

The Ghost of the Boy Who Fell from the Sky

The 78th Police Precinct, located at 65 6th Avenue, is the site of a peculiar haunting. This police station, as is not uncommon given the nature of world, is a place where people have died, prisoners have attempted suicide and distraught spirits linger. There are, in other words, a good number of instances of paranormal activity.

It is thought that these ghosts have now become more active. Some psychics believe the construction of the Nets arena a block away has animated them. They have grown curious about the changes in the neighborhood. It is, psychics suggest, the reason these spectral beings have become more visible.

It is not any of the ghosts *inside* the 79th Police Precinct that concerns this haunting, but rather it is the Ghost of the Boy Who Fell from the Sky. The Ghost of the Boy Who Fell from the Sky makes his way to the police station to report his

He is holding his boarding pass for United Airlines flight 826 and a luggage claim ticket.

luggage is lost. He doesn't know where to find it.

He is believed to be the ghost of the one surviving passenger—a young boy—who fell from the sky when United Airlines flight 826 and Trans World Airlines

Newspaper photograph of the wreckage of the midair collision of United Airlines and TWA jetliners on December 16, 1960.

flight 266 collided over Brooklyn on December 16, 1960. United Airlines flight 826, with 84 passengers and crew aboard, departed Chicago O'Hare and was bound for New York Idlewild International Airport (now renamed John F. Kennedy International Airport). It crashed

in Park Slope along Sterling Place and 7th Avenue. Trans World Airlines flight 266, with 44 passengers and crew aboard was scheduled to land at LaGuardia Airport, arriving from Dayton and Columbus, Ohio. It crashed into a vacant airfield, now part of Gateway National Park, on Staten Island. The disaster killed all 128 people aboard both aircraft and six people on the ground.

One passenger survived the initial impact. Stephen L. Baltz, an 11-year-old boy from Wilmette, Illinois, was thrown from the tail section of the United Airlines jetliner and landed on a snow bank. Residents rolled him in the snow to extinguish the flames that engulfed his clothes. He was conscious, and Dorothy M. Fletcher, who lived at 143 Berkeley Place, rushed to help. The photograph of her holding an umbrella to protect the child from the falling snow made headlines around the country.

In 2004, at the age of 91, she was interviewed by Nathaniel Altman of the *Park Slope Reader*. This is how she recalled that day:

There were two men walking by, and I called out to them, "Do you have a car?" Because there were so many people around there, and so many automobiles that ambulances couldn't get through. And they said, "Yes, we have a car." It was on Lincoln Place. … We lay Stephen on the back seat and I knelt down beside him. All the way up to the hospital he talked to me. What broke my heart was when he asked me if he was going to die. I said, "Not if we can help it. We're taking you to Methodist Hospital." And he said, "That's good, because I am a Methodist." He also told us that his daddy was still in Illinois, in Chicago, and his mother and sister were waiting for him at the airport. They were going to spend Christmas with his uncle up in Yonkers. It's almost as though he were talking to me now. I can hear him. … Up to three years ago, Mrs. Baltz and I sent each other Christmas cards and would report what was going on with our families. And then it stopped like that, and I just surmised that she had passed away.

The boy died from his injuries the following day, peacefully, with his mother and father by his side.

In the intervening decades, there have been reports of the Ghost of the Boy Who Fell from the Sky making his way from the intersection of Sterling Place and 7th Avenue to the 78th Precinct at 65 6th Avenue to report his lost luggage.

Is the Ghost of the Boy Who Fell from the Sky none other than Stephen L. Baltz, the 11-year-old Boy Scout from Illinois, who was flying to New York to spend Christmas with family in Yonkers?

There is a consensus that the ghost is indeed that of Stephen L. Baltz. He is seen wandering the streets. He is holding his boarding pass for United Airlines flight 826 and a luggage claim ticket. He says he is confused, and doesn't know where the airport baggage claim is located. He is sure his mother is waiting

The 78th Police Precinct, located at 65 6th Avenue

for him at the end of the jet way, but he doesn't remember how he got here.

The Ghost of the Boy Who Fell from the Sky has communicated with psychics to let them know that he's a Boy Scout and knows First Aid. He says he can help the injured. The Ghost of the Boy Who Fell from the Sky further claims that when he arrives at the 78th Precinct, the police officers ignore him.

Is it because he's a minor and his parents aren't with him? Is it because they don't believe him when he explains that his airplane crashed a few blocks away? Is it because they don't have time for him?

The Ghost of the Boy Who Fell from the Sky claims he becomes exasperated at being ignored. He leaves the station and just sits on the steps. He wonders what Yummy Tacos are. He is curious—but a bit scared—to go into Hungry Ghost. He only has 65 cents, so he can't even buy a can of soda at the corner store.

The police officers at the 78th Police Precinct may not see or believe the Ghost of the Boy Who Fell from the Sky, but do you?

Do you see him as he approaches the 78th Police Precinct? Do you see him when he's sitting on the steps? Do you see him as he walks the streets, holding his boarding pass, baggage claim ticket and 65 cents?

Do you believe the Ghost of the Boy Who Fell from the Sky when he claims to have fallen from the sky over Park Slope?

In your life, when was the last time you fell and depended on the kindness of strangers?

The Ghost of the Withering Oasis of Lost Time

It stands as a testament to all that could be and what once was. But in the present, it is in a state of unfortunate disrepair.

It is the house at 87 6th Avenue. There has long been confusion about the haunting at this location. For years it was believed there were twin vampires who resided beneath the basement of the structure. It was said that these twins were made into vampires on the same night, and by the same vampire. In consequence, it was speculated that these vampires were benign, meaning they did not feed on the living, because they were able to feed on each other.

The notion that this place was possessed by twins who were also mutual blood-sucking vampires fueled the imagination of nearby residents.

Did they rise at night, suck blood from each other's wrists and return to slumber? Or did they wander the streets supplementing their dietary requirements by feeding on small mammals and domestic pets?

It turns out this speculation was mistaken. It turns out that the house is a place where Santería rituals unfold—performed by the ghost of

There has long been confusion about this haunting. For years it was believed there were twin vampires who resided beneath the basement of the structure.

Is this the residence of the Ghost of Bertrand Alexis?

Bertrand Alexis. He was a Santero who lived in the basement apartment of this property in the 1960s. He refers to this building as the Withering Oasis of Lost Time.

The history of Santería reflects the fusion of West African religious traditions and Spanish Catholicism in the Spanish possessions throughout the Caribbean. As Ernesto Pichardo described in his discussion, "Santería in Contemporary Cuba," at the Third Annual South Florida Symposium on Cuba:

The colonial period from the standpoint of African slaves may be defined as a time of perseverance. Their world quickly changed. Tribal kings and their families, politicians, business and community leaders all were enslaved and taken to a foreign region of the world. Religious leaders, their relatives and their followers were now slaves. Colonial laws criminalized their religion. They were forced to become baptized and worship a god their ancestors had not known who was surrounded by a pantheon of saints. The early concerns during this period seem to have necessitated a need for individual survival under harsh plantation conditions. A sense of hope was sustaining the internal essence of what today is called Santería, a misnomer (and former pejorative) for the indigenous religion of the Lukumi people of Nigeria.

In the heart of their homeland, they had a complex political and

social order. They were a sedentary hoe farming cultural group with specialized labor. Their religion, based on the worship of nature, was renamed and documented by their masters. Santería, a pejorative term that characterizes deviant Catholic forms of worshiping saints, has become a common name for the religion. The term santero(a) is used to describe a priest or priestess replacing the traditional term Olorisha as an extension of the deities. The orishas became known as the saints in image of the Catholic pantheon.

It is in this house that the ghost of the Santero Bertrand Alexis celebrates traditional rituals and plays music in honor of the Orishas. These ceremonies, known as *bembe* or *toque de santo*, consist of the ritual playing of *batá* drums. It is

through the sound of these drums that the messages, prayers and supplications of worshippers reach the Orishas. And it is in the rhythm of the music that the Orishas respond.

The ghost of the Santero Bertrand Alexis claims that he has consistently willed authenticity to the area.

Is this why there is a Cuban restaurant nearby? Is this why there is a Caribbean eatery close at hand? Has the ghost of the Santero Bertrand Alexis "willed" Cubana Café and Sugarcane to the area? Or is this the work of other ghosts that haunt 6th Avenue?

The ghost of the Santero Bertrand Alexis, who refers to himself as the Eternal Guardian of the Withering Oasis of Lost Time, claims the slow beating of drums is like the rhythm of the

human heart, waiting for prayers to be answered. The Eternal Guardian of the Withering Oasis of Lost Time believes the time is at hand for the Great Revelation.

Is it true?

Do you believe it? Can this place be the spot where humanity will recover its Lost Time?

What would you do with if you were given the opportunity to recover the time you have squandered away?

Who wouldn't want to regain lost time? Who wouldn't want to recover time squandered?

What would you do with time regained?

If you know, you are welcome to so inform the Orishas through supplications conveyed by way of *batá* drums.

The Ghost of Mrs. Osborne

It is almost as if she refuses to remain in oblivion. Julia Osborne, the wife of the esteemed Charles W. Osborne, died on July 16, 1918 of what is recorded as hemorrhaging of the pancreas.

She is seen wandering the streets near the Old First Reformed Church, up and down Carroll Street between 6ᵗʰ and 7ᵗʰ Avenues. She lived for more than two decades on Carroll Street, and, along with her husband, was a member of this church.

She is seen clutching her rib cage, as if in pain. Some witnesses report seeing blood seeping through her white nightgown. Others report that it looks like a hospital gown, and is stainless.

Russell Sage, whom Mrs. Julia Osborne secretly loved

What can be said with confidence is that, in the few times she has spoken, she has not mentioned her husband's name. She speaks the name of another man: Russell Sage.

Yes, it's *that* Russell Sage. It is the Russell Sage for whom her husband worked for as a private secretary. It is the Russell Sage who was a successful financier, a railroad executive and an aspiring politician for the Whig Party. It is the Russell Page for whom Russell Sage College is named and whose fortune provided the endowment for the Russell Sage Foundation.

She is seen clutching her rib cage, as if in pain. Some witnesses report seeing blood seeping through her white nightgown.

It is said that in life Julia Osborne longed in her heart for Mr. Russell Sage's touch. It is believed that she loved him from afar, only encountering him on occasion, when her husband met with him or at social events in Manhattan. It is said that Julia Osborne confided the conflicts in her heart—torn between devotion to her husband and the carnal lust she felt for Mr. Russell Sage—to the Reverend James M. Farral.

Reverend Farral reminded Julia Osborne that Matthew 5:27-28 says this of Lust:

Ye have heard that it was said by them of old time, Thou shalt not commit adultery: But I say unto you, That whosoever looketh on a woman to lust after her hath committed adultery with her already in his heart.

Julia Osborne replied that if she already committed a sin in her heart, why couldn't she enjoy the pleasure of the sin in her loins?

Enraged at the audacity of such a statement, the Reverend Farral replied: "Perhaps the Lord will meet you halfway!"

It was then that Julia Osborne began to suffer from discomfort in her pancreas.

What is one to make of this? Is it possible that her lust for a man provoked her illness? Is her

presence in the neighborhood the distraught wanderings of regret?

What if she had touched Mr. Russell Sage's hand when she was in his presence? What if she had dared confess her feelings for him? Is that the reason she is here among the living? Because of regret?

Is that what awaits those who live with regret, who suppress their passion, whose prudence undermines their personal fulfillment?

As you walk the streets

The ghost of Mrs. Julia Osborne haunts the streets near the Old First Reformed Church in Park Slope.

around Carroll Street between 6ᵗʰ and 7ᵗʰ Avenues, are there any longings and cravings in your heart that you dare not act upon?

If so, why not?

Are you prepared to join Mrs. Osborne and spend an afterlife in limbo, torn between the regrets of this world and the helplessness of the next?

Is averting a sin worth an afterlife of regret?

What say you?

The Soul of the Jamaican Nanny

For years there has been speculation. For years people in Park Slope debated what it meant. There was a stroller. There were flowers. The stroller, painted white, had been abandoned. It was an odd sight, and this in a neighborhood where the odd coexists with the pedestrian without much comment. It was christened "The Ghost Stroller."

The stroller first appeared on the corner of Union Street and 6th Avenue. Then it was moved one block away to Berkely Street and 6th Avenue. It even garnered the interest of the *New York Times*.

"Sometimes the passers-by look curious; sometimes they are distraught, concerned by the three plastic roses—peach, pink and red—tucked behind the straps, which give the stroller the distinct look of a memorial commemorating some grim accident," reporter Susan Dominus wrote back in 2010.

The stroller was. The stroller is.

The stroller is a reminder of the ghost of the Jamaican Nanny's presence in Park Slope. The stroller was created by the

It is one thing to cast a spell, but it is another thing to unleash malevolent spirits upon one's sibling.

ghost of the Jamaican Nanny to honor the child in her care at the time of her abduction. The stroller is a *memento mori* of a promise broken, but only because she could not keep the

promise made.

The soul of the Jamaican Nanny is Emerald Dixon, a young Jamaican woman who arrived in Brooklyn in 2004, at the age of 23. Her dream was to complete her studies and become a licensed nurse in the United States. She supported herself by taking care of the white and biracial children of privileged families in Park Slope. She studied at night. She was a full-

time nanny and a part-time student.

She was also bewitched. A spell had been cast on her by a jealous sister, one who was enraged that she had been unable to journey to the United States to conclude her own studies. Her sister resented that she remained behind in Kingston.

It is one thing to cast a spell, however, and it is another thing to unleash malevolent spirits upon one's sibling. Without realizing it, by casting that spell, Emerald Dixon's own sister unleashed Duppies into Brooklyn!

What is a Duppy, you ask?

If you have to ask, then there is a tremendous gap in your knowledge of Caribbean folklore and the religious traditions of the African diaspora in the Caribbean, gentle reader. Not to worry, however. This is an opportune moment to remedy that situation. In Jamaican Patois, a Duppy, a word derived from the languages spoken in northwest Africa, is a malevolent spirit that haunts and torments the living.

It is believed the soul of the Jamaican nanny creates "ghost strollers" that have been seen in Park Slope periodically.

In the Obea religion, a common faith popular among the African diaspora throughout the Caribbean nations that were under English colonial rule, it is believed that humans possess two souls. (In the Lesser Antilles, Duppies are Jumbies.) There is the heavenly soul, which ascends to heaven upon death to be judged by God. There is also an earthly soul, one that remains on Earth for three days with the body. If care is not taken, it is this soul that can escape one's coffin, and wander the Earth as a Duppy.

Duppies are in fact the malevolent souls of the recently-dead that escaped unguarded coffins. In casting her spell, Emerald Dixon's sister unwittingly allowed three Duppies to escape the funeral home where she worked in Kingston as an administrative assistant.

These Duppies, set loose upon the world, were caught in the spiritual vortex of the spell cast and were transported to Brooklyn. They appeared one evening while Emerald Dixon was with the young child in her care. These Duppies descended upon the Jamaican nanny and tore her to pieces, devouring her limbs with voracious hunger. There was nothing left of Emerald Dixon, except for her soul, which managed to ascend to heaven.

Her earthly soul, on the hand, the one that never received a proper funeral and burial escaped into Park Slope. It is this soul that painted the stroller white and placed the plastic flowers in it. The white represents the color of a nurse's uniform. The roses are the flowers no one ever placed on her own tomb. The intersection is one that, in life, she crossed every day in the course of her being a nanny to a child born into a family of privilege.

From time to time the soul of the Jamaican Nanny will leave a stroller in Park Slope to remind the people of Brooklyn of her dedication to the children for whom she cared. Strollers have been seen on 8th Avenue and 11th Street and on Prospect Park West and 10th Street.

Do you see that other nanny pushing a stroller

with a child not her own? If she is taking care of your child, who is taking care of hers? Does she remind you of somebody that you used to know? Does she remind you of the love, loyalty and dedication of Emerald Dixon?

Is that stroller there to remind you that you can't pretend that it never happened?

Does the soul of the Jamaican Nanny want to warn you of the Duppies now set loose in Park Slope?

The Soul in Search of His Twin

It is no secret that gemellology, the scientific term for the study of twins, has long confirmed what most people intuitively understand: identical twins share a bond that defies what can otherwise be explained as coincidence.

Now consider the case of Patrick Hearn, a 22-year-old young man who served his country during World War I. Patrick—known as Paddy—enlisted, along with his identical twin, Mac, to fight in the Great War. The Hearn brothers were immigrants from Ballinrole, Ireland. They arrived in Brooklyn as young boys, with the full expectation that they, along with their family, would have better lives in this country. He and his family lived at 214 6th Avenue, between Union and President Streets.

War, however, upended their dreams. The Hearn brothers found themselves serving in Company C of the 69th Regiment. It was an ordeal of unimaginable brutality. Conditions on the front being what they were, many young men succumbed to injuries, infection and disease.

On July 11, 1918, news reached Brooklyn that Paddy Hearn had died, a consequence of disease. The news tore asunder the Hearn family. They feared the same fate would fall their other son. The family's grief was complete. The mother was inconsolable. She

There have been reports of Paddy Hearn's soul sitting on the steps to his former residence...

availed herself to séances to reach out to her lost boy.

In journal entries she described the solemnity of the gathering at her home, and how

Once seen by the Carroll Park War Memorial, the ghost of Paddy Hearn today lingers near his residence, 214 6th Avenue, where he waits for his twin brother.

those present at the séance felt a presence fill the room. They held hands and concentrated their thoughts and prayers on reaching Paddy Hearn. Her journal described the confusing number of fallen soldiers from the carnage of the Great War they reached. "I am not certain of the identities of the spirits we

contacted," she wrote in a letter to a friend in Boston. "But we are confident that we will soon contact my lad, my beloved Paddy." Mrs. Hearn held three additional séances in her home, but none concluded to her satisfaction.

Since that time, however, there have been reports of Paddy Hearn's soul sitting on the steps to his former residence. It is said that he is waiting for his brother Mac. It is said that he just wants to be home, but doesn't understand where everyone has gone.

"I'm not sure why my keys don't work," his soul answers when asked why he is sitting on the stoop. "I'm sure my brother will be back soon."

Psychics who have made contact with him report that Paddy Hearn is happy he left the war without becoming a "basket case," which was a term first employed during World War I to denote a person who, because he had lost all four limbs, had to be carried in a basket.

"I'm glad I made it home safely," the soul of Paddy Hearn says, apparently unaware he is dead. "But I don't know why my brother is not back."

You, gentle reader, understand fully well he didn't make it home safely. You, gentle reader, understand why his keys from 1918 won't open the front door today.

Would you be able to explain the reason to the forlorn Paddy Hearn?

The Ghost of the Suffragette

On warm summer evenings, there are reports of a woman's voice heard in the area surrounding the Bailey Fountain at Grand Army Plaza. At times it sounds as if the woman is whispering, softly reciting a prayer. On other occasions she is said to sound as if in a trance, repeating a mantra. Always, however, the phrases heard are consistent: *repeated injuries … usurpations on the part of man … tyranny over her …*

It was only after several attempts to reach this voice—she

Many believe that Elizabeth Cady Stanton lingers at the Bailey Fountain, repeating her mantra.

is heard but is seldom seen—did her entire incantation become apparent. The ghost repeats this one sentence and one sentence alone: "The history of mankind is a history of repeated injuries and usurpations on the part of man toward woman, having in direct object the establishment of an absolute tyranny over her."

Who is she? What does this mean? Why is she here at Bailey Fountain?

The answers uncovered are tantalizing.

That sentence is part of the "Declaration of Sentiments," written by Elizabeth Cady Stanton in 1848. This declaration was part of a document signed by participants of the Seneca Falls Convention that same year. This was the first women's rights gathering in the United States. Elizabeth Cady Stanton was an early suffragette who advocated the establishment of a broad social program to grant women all the political and economic

Is the ghost that lingers near Bailey Fountain at Grand Army Plaza that of Elizabeth Cady Stanton?

rights that men enjoyed.

When one considers that this was a time when the nation struggled with the question of slavery—the Civil War would erupt 13 years after this statement was signed—the participants of the Seneca Falls Convention were ahead of their time. Indeed, it would be 72 years after the Senecal Falls Convention before the 19th amendment was ratified in 1920 establishing universal suffrage in the United States.

Could the ghost be none other than Elizabeth Cady Stanton?

She has not revealed her name when asked. She simply repeats the same sentence. But there is a strong likelihood that the "Ghost of the Suffragette" is, in fact, Elizabeth Cady Stanton.

Bailey Fountain was built by Frank Bailey, a 19th century financier and philanthropist. Frank Bailey began his career as a clerk at the Title Guarantee and Trust Company and rose to become its president. Bailey's family had a long history of social activism. His father, Dr. William Cady Bailey, opened his home to runaway slaves. The elder Bailey residence was a clandestine station on the Underground Railroad. On his mother's side, social activism was very much in evidence: Elizabeth Cady Stanton was a relative!

She considered Frank Bailey to be her nephew—they were distant cousins, a generation apart. She encouraged him to cultivate social consciousness. In his later years—Frank Bailey died in 1953—he lamented that Elizabeth Cady Stanton did not live to see women get the right to vote, which came true 18 years after her death.

Frank Bailey remembered that, while he may have built the fountain as a memorial to his wife, Marie Louise Eastman, it was Elizabeth Cady Stanton who taught him the importance of

giving back to society. It was an obligation that his "aunt"

She has not revealed her name when asked. She simply repeats the same sentence.

inculcated in him. Indeed, Frank Bailey sat on the boards of the Museum of the City of New York; the Brooklyn Institute of Arts and Sciences; and the Brooklyn Botanic Garden.

Is it possible that Elizabeth Cady Stanton has chosen to enjoy this splendid spot, built by her "nephew," to bear witness to the social strides women have made?

She is largely credited with encouraring Frank Bailey's parents of "living" their "Christian faith" by working to end human bondage. As an abolitionist herself, she was relentless in her work. After the Civil War, she joined others to work for the establishment of the same rights for all the disenfranchised: African-Americans and women.

One psychic who made contact with the ghost claims she expressed "pride" in the work of her "nephew" and in the steady advancement of women in the United States. One clairvoyant sensed her "pride" in eavesdropping on Nina Totenberg's reporting on legal affairs on NPR, as well as her delight in listening to the interviews on "Fresh Air" with Terry Gross. This was without this psychic or clairvoyant being told anything else about this fountain. Many believe that Elizabeth Cady Stanton lingers at the Bailey Fountain, repeating her mantra as a reminder to the living of the work that still remains undone.

Listen carefully! Do you hear her words across the waves of time? Is her plea as eternal and beautiful as a spray of water from a glorious fountain on a summer day?

Is that why she is here?

To remind you of the work that remains to be done in the name of what is just? To encourage you to seize the promise of summertime to work for good?

Is it to remind you that the light of day is the time to work for good?

The Mischievous Leprechauns of Montauk Club

It is, by all accounts, an amusing haunting. Some say it's not even a haunting. Then again, who's to say if the presence of three leprechauns dancing on the roof of the Montauk Club is something to be feared?

What can be said with certainty is that there are three leprechauns atop the Montauk Club on 8th Avenue.

These are neither dwarves nor midgets, mind you. They are leprechauns who spend their days mending the shoes they find along the streets of Brooklyn. As dusk settles, they will, when provoked, hurl shoes at pedestrians below.

There are three leprechauns dancing and carrying on atop the roof of the Montauk Club.

What can be said of low creatures?

Have you forgotten? Don't you remember the description of leprechauns in *Irish Wonders* by D. R. McAnally? In it he writes:

By birth the Leprechaun is of low descent, his father being an evil spirit and his mother a degenerate fairy; by nature he is a mischief-maker, the Puck of the Emerald Isle. He is of diminutive size, about three feet high, and is dressed in a little red jacket or roundabout, with red breeches buckled at the knee, gray or black stockings, and a hat, cocked in the style of a century ago, over a little, old, withered face. Round his neck is an Elizabethan ruff, and frills of lace are at his wrists. On the wildest coast, where the Atlantic winds bring almost

The Montauk Club in Park Slope

constant rains, he dispenses with ruff and frills and wears a frieze overcoat over his pretty red suit, so that, unless on the lookout for the cocked hat, "ye might pass a Leprechawn on the road and never know it's himself that's in it at all."

As is often the case in life, leprechauns are neither good, nor evil. They just are.

There has long been speculation why these three leprechauns, who are dressed in their traditional red—not green—coats, arrived at the Montauk Club. It was by invitation: the founders of the Club gave them permission to live there!

Charles Pratt and Edwin Litchfield, along with Richard Schermerhorn and Francis Kimball, were among the founding members of the Montauk Club. Legend has it that Charles Pratt and Edwin Litchfield, while surveying the vast tract of land between what is now the Montauk Club and the Gowanus Canal, came upon a leprechaun in distress. Rather than attacking the defenseless creature, they acted as Good Samaritans and offered assistance. The leprechaun was so grateful, that he granted the men three wishes.

This might be an opportune moment to point out that, according to Irish folklore, leprechauns have the power to grant wishes. Indeed, history recounts the story of Fergus Mac Léti, King of Ulster, who, falling asleep on the beach one day suddenly awoke to find himself seized upon and being dragged by three leprechauns! In a fierce struggle Mac Léti overpowered the leprechauns. These creatures were stunned by Mac Léti's skills at hand-to-hand combat. They made a deal in which each leprechaun granted the king one

wish if the king released all three. And so it was done.

In 1890, only one year after the Montauk Club was founded, when Charles Pratt and Edwin Litchfield came upon the leprechaun in distress, he is said to have been so grateful that he granted the men three wishes. Legend has it that Charles Pratt and Edwin Litchfield conferred and settled upon splitting their wishes in the following manner: Pratt would ask for one thing; Litchfield would ask for another; and the men agreed that the third wish would revert back to the leprechaun.

It is said that the leprechaun was so taken by this kindness that he burst into tears!

Pratt wished that the educational institution he had founded would prosper, and so would his own fortune. This wish was granted: Pratt Institute remains a renowned art college, and his business dealings with John D. Rockefeller prospered. Litchfield wished for the continued success of the development of the lands where today Prospect Park, Park Slope and Gowanus Canal are located. These neighborhoods have become among the most prized areas of the greater New York metropolitan region through the

Charles Pratt and Edwin Litchfield, while surveying the vast tract of land between the Montauk Club and the Gowanus Canal, came upon a leprechaun in distress.

fortunes and misfortunes, ups and downs of the New York economy over the course of more than a century.

What of the leprechaun's own wish?

Legend has it the leprechaun lamented that his kind was a solitary creature. It proved draining on one's spirit to be so alone in the world. He wished he could live in the company of his brothers so that each might comfort the other, and offer assistance as they lived their lives through the ages.

Neither man objected to such a wish.

So it was made, and so it was granted. This is the reason there are three leprechauns dancing and carrying on atop the roof of the Montauk Club. This is the reason they roam the neighborhood, scavenging shoes to mend. This is the reason that in the evenings they amuse themselves by hurling shoes at pedestrians below. (They are often seen at the back of the Montauk Club, where Lincoln Place and Plaza Street West converge.) They are more active when the Montauk Club holds events for singles, and when the Corduroy Club has its meetings.

Should you find yourself strolling along Plaza Street West and think you hear the high-pitched laughter of little people, you're not imagining things. Should you see a hurled shoe fly across the sidewalk, you're not imagining things. Should you see the silhouettes of three diminutive men running along the roof of the Montauk Club, you're not imagining things.

These are the leprechauns of Park Slope. They are there with the permission of Charles Pratt and Edwin Litchfield.

They have as much right to be up there as anyone!

Remember that. They have as much right to hurl a shoe at you as anyone else has a right to hurl a shoe at you.

God knows there are lots of people who claim the right to want to hurl a shoe at you!

The Ghost at Mrs. Maxwell's House of English Vices

A long the streets of Park Slope, not far from Prospect Park, on 2nd Street between 8th Avenue and Prospect Park West, is a most intriguing haunting. It is a haunting more of a sensory experience than of a spiritual essence. It is one of energy, sensuality and life that is so thrilling that the current residents have requested that the exact street address not be published. They do not want to be inundated—even more than

Some see the apparition of a woman who bears a striking resemblance to John Singer Sargent's portrait of Madame X.

they already are—by those seeking the titillation and exhilaration of the English vice.

What is the English vice you ask?

If you have to ask, then it

probably is not one of your … *sexual desires*. Then again, it might just be, but you just don't know it yet.

That's often the case in life, isn't it? You don't know you will like something until you try it. Didn't your mother use to say that? Of course she was probably referring to eating broccoli and not … *sexual fetishes*.

"Now dear, how do you know you don't like broccoli unless you try it?" is more often

To this day, some young women who linger near Mrs. Maxwell's House of English Vices claim to experience spontaneous orgasms!

heard coming out of the mouths of mothers than, "Now dear, how do you know you won't achieve spontaneous orgasm during a round of vigorous bare-ass spanking until you try it."

That's the English vice! Spanking for sexual pleasure!

Mrs. Maxwell is the name of the woman who satisfied the Victorian and Edwardian demand for discretion when indulging the English vice.

"He delicately edged her knickers down using the tips of his thumb and forefinger," Jenny Diski wrote in her novel, *Nothing Natural*, published in 1986.

There is something to be said for certain cravings, distinct desires, and longings that linger in the mind. Silver screen images flicker with visions of a deeply pleasurable sense of exposure and humiliation at the prospect of a strong slap across an ass. How many films portrayed John Wayne smacking some actress across the ass by way of establishing the terms of their relationship? More than Netflix can keep on hand.

If you imagine these kinds of dreams … then you are on the right street in Brooklyn.

"There is a deep arousing sensation that wells up inside my entire body when you firmly tell me you are going to spank me," one man wrote to Mrs. Maxwell in 1905. "It is as much sexual in origin, as it is emotional, I'm afraid. Yes, my mistress, the sexual aspect of the encounter has as much to do with being naked before you, lying prostate over your knee, the scent of your perfumed dress filling my head as I await the pleasurable pain you are about to deliver. I confess it is thrilling to know you are admiring my bare bottom and I am vulnerable before you, as it is about the anticipation of the spanking itself. There is also the

knowledge that your firm hands will touch my bare-ass, that the back of your brush will smack my buttocks as you hold me firmly down. I know that we shall share loving feelings towards each other when the session is over."

In his book, *Confessions*, Jean-Jacques Rousseau similarly described his pleasure at being spanked. In more recent times, Peter Lawford, the actor and brother-in-law of John F. Kennedy, shared similar fetishes. Lawford regaled with his tales of the arousal he derived when he was spanked, and he boasted of the sexual habits of his Hollywood friends. "The burning on my ass is pleasant when I am spanked properly," he said. "If it is tender the next day, then I will be happy. If I see redness on my buttocks when I look in the mirror, that alone I find arousing. I enjoy looking at the redness, and I enjoy it when I am spanked again. It seldom hurts the second time; my ass is numb to the touch but the second spanking keeps my ass warm." (Lawford recounted that, then-B-movie actress, Nancy Davis was renowned for performing among the best

Mrs. Maxwell, a proper Edwardian woman, whose given name was Mayyada, which in Arabic means a woman who walks with a proud strut, understood the nature of this fetish.

fellatio in Hollywood after she was subjected to a vigorous round of bare-ass spanking.) Andy Warhol claimed that the sexual pleasure he most enjoyed was watching a man being spanked by a drag queen, while both were high on speed. The English vice has many adherents.

Mrs. Maxwell, a proper Edwardian woman, whose given name was Mayyada, which in

Arabic means a woman who walks with a proud strut, understood the nature of this fetish. She understood the psychological desire that was self-evident when hand met the bare flesh of a grown man's or grown woman's buttocks.

"It cannot be denied that these desires are simply the stating and restating, in an adult arena, of the emotionally vulnerable condition of childhood," she wrote one supplicant who stated she would pay any price for being brutalized the way her husband refused ever to do. "It is a perfectly acceptable vanity, my dear. It is the acceptance that, at times, under certain circumstances, the emotional condition of childhood is reliving conditional pain as the price for unconditional love. I shall be delighted to indulge your wish to be loved through the pain of the English vice, and in the process I have no doubt you shall enjoy vigorous orgasms that approximate spiritual ecstasy. Present yourself with this letter at my House of English Vices on the 30th of June and expect to remain here until the 2nd of July."

These are the kinds of notes, letters and journal entries that were located in the attic of the residence in question in the 1960s.

There was also an invitation that was sent to 35 individuals for a fete she hosted in 1910. The engraved invitation reads: "Mrs. Maxwell's House of English Vices: A Dispirited and Distasteful Diversion for Christmas." If this sounds familiar, it should: decades later Edward Gorey wrote a book, *The Haunted Tea-Cosy: A Dispirited and Distasteful Diversion for Christmas*, after he found one invitation (used as a bookmark) in a book he shoplifted from the Strand Book Store.

With this background, we can now proceed to the nature of this haunting.

For decades, some individuals have reported that, when lingering in front of the houses numbering between 630 and 640 of that block, they have felt a slight burning sensation on their buttocks. Others note that, when returning home, they undress and, upon examination, see the slight outline of a handprint on their buttocks. A few women, usually aged between 24 and 35, report spontaneous orgasms if they stand and linger on the sidewalk for more than a few minutes.

There are those who see the apparition of a woman who bears a striking resemblance to John Singer Sargent's portrait of Madame X. Everyone knows Madame X was, in fact, Madame Pierre Gautreau. Psychics who have attempted to make contact with the ghost at Mrs. Maxwell's House of English Vices insist that the apparition claims that she is Mayyada Maxwell. She claims that it was none other Madame Pierre Gautreau who adopted *her* style as her own—after the latter traveled to New York to be spanked! Madame Pierre Gautreau was Virginie Amélie Avegno Gautreau, an American socialite born in New Orleans, whose family fled to France to escape the American Civil War. (In 1862 her father, Anatole Placide Avegno, died from injuries sustained during the Battle of Shiloh.) Madame X grew to loathe the country of her birth for what it did to her father.

Did Mrs. Maxwell spank Madame X? There is no known record of her having traveled to New York to indulge in the English vice.

Neighbors say that those who desire to indulge the English vice are drawn to the neighborhood. There are those who claim that visitors to this street are disproportionately inclined to indulge in this fetish. There are some who say that the street is filled with sexual fantasists.

One woman wrote Mrs. Maxwell the following letter after a summer-long retreat at Mrs. Maxwell's House of English Vices, a summer that was characterized by nightly spankings. The year was 1908. "I need your touch," the grateful woman wrote. "I recognize total surrender leaves me vulnerable, but it is a vulnerability that leaves me tender. I want you to hold me tightly, my precious Mrs. Maxwell. I long for the embrace of your arms around me. The thought of your hands on my waist brings me to tears, and I feel a spiritual connection to you. After you spank me and I stand naked before you, I am at peace and I am calm and I am freed of the hysterics that otherwise overpower me. It is only then that I experience calm and I can radiate a joyful existence. I do not know if you have saved my soul, but you have indeed saved my life by giving me sanity."

Is a sound spanking a cure for modern neurosis?

Are you prepared? Are you willing to submit yourself to the hand that strikes a bare-ass? Are you prepared to walk down this street and run the risk of a spontaneous orgasm that often accompanies one of Mrs. Maxwell's vigorous spankings?

Look up!

Is that her by the window? Does she resemble a John Singer Sargent portrait? Is she slowly moving the curtains to gaze upon you, spanking submissive? Are you among those willing to submit to the pleasures contained within Mrs. Maxwell's House of English Vices?

If not, then why are you walking down her street?

"I want you to hold me tightly, my precious Mrs. Maxwell. I long for the embrace of your arms around me."

The Soul of the Cross Dressing Bon Vivant

When you stand before 27 Prospect Park West, one of the first things you should know is that this is one of the few remaining buildings in New York that has an elevator man.

Isn't that swell?

This is a building where a person is employed to take you to your apartment. And what apartments these are! With sweeping views of Prospect Park, spacious rooms in a pre-War building that is unrivaled in elegance, these residences are said to be possessed by a spirit of a live-in guest from decades past.

Clairvoyants who have made contact with the soul believed to inhabit this building see him strut down the streets as he turns the corner with a confident air. They report his name is Thomas Johnson. They say his aunt and uncle resided at 27 Prospect Park West during the 1920s and 1930s. Thomas Johnson frequently spent months with his relatives, grateful that they opened their home to him. They were steadfast in their love for him.

Thomas Johnson, you understand, had been turned out of his own home by his parents. It is his father who asked him to leave the family residence near Gramercy Park in Manhattan. The reason for this expulsion was that Thomas Johnson was transgender.

"I worshipped Gloria Swanson and Louise Brooks," the soul of Thomas Johnson communicates to clairvoyants. "No one was more stylish than Josephine Baker. No one had

His uncle and aunt were not judgmental in his habits, however peculiar they found these to be.

more elegant taste than Coco Chanel."

Thomas Johnson moved in certain circles, those consisting of drag queens and drag kings. He favored fishnet stockings, which were associated with prostitutes in his time. "I didn't

The soul of Thomas Johnson is believed to inhabit this residence on Prospect Park West.

care, and I didn't flaunt these in public—just at the clubs and cabarets," he communicates. "Say what you will, I had discretion."

When the maid found his clandestine collection of women's clothing, shoes and stockings, his father confronted him about the matter. His mother cried. She was so distraught she availed herself to Catholicism: Saint Servatius, the patron saint of feet and legs.

"Our entire family was engulfed in turmoil!" Thomas Johnson communicates. "We were a proper Protestant family, and there was my mother reciting Catholic prayers to Saint Servatius to cure me of whatever condition I had that made me long for women's shoes, stockings, leggings and dresses. My father was ashamed of me. And it was to avoid this shame and scandal that he asked me to leave."

Thomas Johnson found refuge and acceptance in Brooklyn. His uncle and aunt opened their home to him. They were not judgmental in their nephew's habits, however peculiar they found these to be. They loved him. They welcomed him into their gracious home without condition.

Truth be told, they did enjoy the amusing and clever friends

he had—and the music these acquaintances brought into their home. The sounds of the age filled their home, and the liveliness of American Jazz filled their lives.

Did Thomas Johnson's mother pray to Saint Servatius, the Patron Saint of feet and legs, to cure his son of cross-dressing?

Thomas Johnson, however, was murdered in 1955. He was the victim of "rough trade," a euphemism for a sexual encounter with a paid hustler that turned violent. That was not uncommon in an age when non-heterosexuals lived hidden lives.

In the decades that followed, it is said that the soul of Thomas Johnson walks these familiar streets. Some see him sashay as he leaves 27 Prospect Park West, dressed in Coco Chanel. Others see him meander down the street in the manner reminiscent of

Gloria Swanson at the height of her powers.

When asked what he makes of the world today, he replies that the apogee of acceptance, as he defines it, happened when Lou Reed penned the lyrics to "Walk on the Wild Side."

"Hey babe, take a Walk on the Wild Side," the soul of Thomas Johnson communicates as if in song. "This is what freedom is about! This is what we tried to live when I was alive! This is what keeps me here in this world!"

It is said that the energy and vitality of the soul of Thomas Johnson calls out to kindred spirits. It is said that residents of this building are inclined to indulge in similar fetishes. It is said male residents are known to wear fishnet stockings—and to Walk on the Wild Side. It is said that this building, more than others, harbors the soul of exuberance and uninhibited expression.

Can this be true?

Do you find yourself drawn to this building? Do you think those who reside in this building are exuberant and joyful?

Are they inclined to Walk on the Wild Side?

Are you?

The Demonic Possession of Villa Litchfield

I t can be said with certainty that trouble began within a decade after the Italianate mansion was built in 1854 on an estate Edwin Clark Litchfield owned. The Villa, now part of Prospect Park, was designed by Alexander

Porcelain plates fell to the floor and framed pictures crashed to the ground...

Jackson Davis, and it entered the National Register of Historic Places in 1977.

Villa Litchfield, however, is noted—and notorious—as a place of demonic possession. Its top floors are said to be occupied by diabolic familiars. It is said that these appear as gargoyles, peering out the windows, their eyes glowing

Is the Villa Litchfield possessed by demonic gargoyles?

47

green and their tongues a luminescent red. It is believed the demonic possession occurred in the course of a séance that went wrong in 1864.

Legend tells of a certain Mrs. Margaret Cahill, who, distraught over the death of her son on the battlefields of the Civil War, refused to believe she would never see him again in this life. She became an enthusiastic follower of spiritualists who believed it was possible to receive messages from the souls of the dead. She desperately wanted to reach out to her son. She wanted to rest her mind that he was not suffering in the hereafter and that he had forgiven the world for his having been killed at such a tender age.

It was well-known among the public that Mary Todd Lincoln organized séances at the White House, she so grieved the death of her son. It was also well-known that president Abraham Lincoln attended a few of these sessions at the request of the First Lady. It was a common pursuit among women who had lost their fathers, husbands, brothers, or sons to the carnage of war to want to reach out to those lost. In the second half of the 19th century Americans were exhausted and distraught at the loss of life that resulted from the Civil War. They desperately wanted to use mystics and clairvoyants to make contact with the dead.

Mrs. Cahill, who was a friend of Edwin Clark Litchfield, enlisted his permission to arrange for a séance at his home. This session to contact her son's soul proved successful—or at least entertaining enough. In consequence, several other séances were held.

In the course of conducting one such séance, however, something went wrong. Some say her son was confined in Hell, and in communicating with him, demons entered our world. Others believe the séance itself was conducted

Luke 13:10-17

And he was teaching in one of the synagogues on the sabbath.

And, behold, there was a woman which had a spirit of infirmity eighteen years, and was bowed together, and could in no wise lift up herself.

And when Jesus saw her, he called her to him, and said unto her, Woman, thou art loosed from thine infirmity.

And he laid his hands on her: and immediately she was made straight, and glorified God.

And the ruler of the synagogue answered with indignation, because that Jesus had healed on the sabbath day, and said unto the people, There are six days in which men ought to work: in them therefore come and be healed, and not on the sabbath day.

The Lord then answered him, and said, Thou hypocrite, doth not each one of you on the sabbath loose his ox or his ass from the stall, and lead him away to watering?

And ought not this woman, being a daughter of Abraham, whom Satan hath bound, lo, these eighteen years, be loosed from this bond on the sabbath day?

And when he had said these things, all his adversaries were ashamed: and all the people rejoiced for all the glorious things that were done by him.

improperly and that a vortex opened allowing for the demonic possession of Villa Litchfield. A few claim that one of the participants was already possessed by a

demon and that the séance released the demonic presence within her.

It was scandalous. Two authorities on séances claim that Spiritualism can release demonic possession into this world. The Bible was often cited as proof. Back in 1864 Mrs. Cahill believed the gospel according to Luke, which tells the story of Jesus Christ freeing a woman of demonic possession.

Thus emboldened and with complete confidence and faith in the Bible, Mrs. Cahill soldiered on.

Mrs. Cahill was, in fact, so taken by the frenzied nature of the sessions held at Villa Litchfield that they gained notoriety among nearby residents. During the séance in question, the table vibrated, the lights flickered. There was a low rumbling and the air whirled in an inexplicable manner. The shaking intensified to the point that porcelain plates fell to the floor and framed pictures crashed to the ground.

One of the participants— Mrs. Margaret Rossiter— collapsed at the terror of the proceedings. Two others present fled the scene, running from the mansion, screaming in horror. One was almost trampled by a horse-drawn carriage. It is said that the room went completely dark and that demons appeared, instantaneously vanishing through the ceiling and into the upper floors.

Then, as suddenly as it began, it ended.

The lights came back on. The shaking stopped. The scent of sulfur dissipated. It was as if nothing had occurred. Mrs. Rossiter was revived, and the episode was dismissed as a brief fainting

Séances were popular during the Civil War, as desperate relatives sought to make contact with their lost fathers, husbands, brothers and sons. Mary Todd Lincoln organized séances at the White House and President Abraham Lincoln attended a number of them.

present at the séance died within a year. Mr. William Brownell died from injuries sustained from an accidental fall. Mr. George Vonderlin died of a nervous attack. Both Mrs. Cahill and Mrs. Rossiter also died in 1865, and the cause of death for each woman is listed as consumption, a euphemism for untreated tuberculosis.

It is claimed that Edwin Clark Litchfield never sensed the presence of the demonic possession, but that a good number of other people in his household did. It is said he was happy to dispose of the property in 1868 when he sold it to the Brooklyn Parks Commission. (The building is currently occupied by New York City Department of Parks and the offices of the Prospect Park Alliance.) It is said the building remains possessed by demons in the guise of gargoyles, which appear in the windows of the top floors.

It is said that spiritualists are drawn to the area and that residents in the buildings along Prospect Park West between 3rd and 6th Streets include a good number of women who hold séances to this day. It is said that when a séance is held, the demons become more active and agitated, their gargoyle forms cast shadows from the windows.

The demonic possession unleashed by a séance so many decades ago is still very much in evidence.

Do you believe this? Do you see them? Do you sense the demons that occupy the upper floors of the Villa Litchfield?

Do they appear as the grotesque gargoyles they are said to be?

spell preciptated by the emotions of the moment.

The events proved unnerving, however, and the séance came to an abrupt and inconclusive end. In her journal, Mrs. Cahill noted that oftentimes "the grotesque coexists in disharmony with the divine."

Those present claimed that no further contact of any spiritual kind was detected … *until dusk the next day*. That

is when the haunting was first noted. That is when demons resembling gargoyles first appeared in the windows of the Villa Litchfield.

Of the five individuals present that evening for Mrs. Cahill's séance, one, a Mr. William Woodruff, vanished from the historical record completely. (It is said he was seized by the Fallen Angel Lucifer and taken to Hell.) The other four individuals

The Ghost of Girl Who Wanted to Go to the Moon

In his autobiography, *My Life and Work*, published in 1922, Henry Ford, writing about the process of automation in the industrial factory, stated that "You can have any color as long as it's black."

The point he was making was that in order to keep costs low, even the color of the Model T car had to be standardized to just one: black. A consumer could have a Model T car in any color, provided that color was black. That was the only choice, and there were no other options. End of story.

With this in mind, now consider the ghost of a teenage girl said to inhabit Prospect Park. Since the summer of 1970 there have been reports of the ghost of a young girl, believed to be either 14 or 15 years old (she does not know her exact age), who wanders through Prospect Park. She is most often seen near the Kate Wollman Prospect Park Rink. Her clothes are wet. Her hair is wet.

There's good reason: she was drowned.

This is the ghost of a lovely teenage girl who was drowned because she wanted a Model T car in a color other than black. This is the ghost of a lovely teenage girl who was drowned because she wanted to go to the moon. This is the ghost of a lovely teenage girl who believed that she lived in a country where she could grow up to become anything she wanted because she was free to follow her dreams.

She was mistaken. No one can dream of having a Model T

She paid a price for daring to desire something her community deemed unacceptable.

car that is a color other than black. In the world in which she lived, no one can aspire to go to the moon. No one can pursue their dream, unless that dream is to live as you are told.

In life this lovely teenage girl was born to a Hasidic Jewish family. This is a community of Orthodox Jews who structure their lives around the belief that the fundamental nature of Jewish faith resides in Jewish mysticism, or the Kabbalah. Hasidic Jews, whose beliefs were established through the teachings of Rabbi Israel ben Eliezer in the 18th century, have grown in number in Brooklyn.

This minority community within the broader Jewish faith adheres to strict rules that govern the lives of men and women, family and faith. It is a life that demands discipline, and it demands the suppression of individual desire for the sake of tradition.

The Ghost of the Girl Who Wanted to go to the Moon tells of the price paid for daring to desire something her community deemed unacceptable. All she wanted to do was go to the moon. That is to say, she dreamed of becoming an astronaut.

Hasidic Jews lead lives where individuality is discouraged.

This was blasphemy. This was outside the realm of possibilities. As a Hasidic Jewish woman, or *Haredi*, there was a uniform dress code to which she had to adhere. She had to wear long, modest skirts. Sleeves had to cover her elbows (considered sensuous and tempting to men's gaze). Her hands could be visible, but not her ankles or feet. Upon marriage, she would have to wear a scarf, or *tichel*; or, preferably, a wig, or *sheitel*. That marriage would take place between the ages of 17 and 25, and it would arranged by a matchmaker, known as a *shidduch*. She would stay at home, be an obedient wife, have many children and raise those children. As a Hasidic Jewish woman, she would be a wife, a homemaker and a mother.

"I could be anything I wanted, but only if I wanted to be a wife and mother," the Ghost of the Girl Who Wanted to go to the Moon says.

She wanted to study. She wanted to go to college. She wanted to pursue graduate studies. She wanted to work for NASA. She wanted to delay marriage. She wanted to go into outerspace. She wanted the impossible.

These desires led to conflicts and turmoil. She was accused of being immoral and disobedient, unnatural and depraved. She was told her desires dishonored the family and were against the will of God.

"My father told me that he would rather see me dead than dishonor the community," she conveys to psychics.

In the same way that Henry Ford would sell you a Model T car in any color you wanted, provided you wanted the color black, Rabbi Israel ben Eliezer would give you whatever dream you wanted, provided your dream was his shade of Judaism.

The Ghost of the Girl Who Wanted to go to the Moon tells how she read about the moon landing. The Ghost of the Girl Who Wanted to go to the Moon tells of her excitement in dreaming this could be her reality as well. The Ghost of the Girl Who Wanted to go to the

The girl dreamed about a lunar landing such as this.

Moon also tells about the night when the world celebrated the first anniversary of Neil Armstrong walking on the surface of the moon.

There are dreams that life cannot weather.

And so, on July 20, 1970, her father ordereds her to accompany him for a walk. She obeyed. They walked to Prospect Park and made their way to Prospect Park Lake, a short distance from the skating rink.

All that spring she had talked of nothing but studying and going to college. She had fantasized about graduate studies, the physical training and the rigorous standards demanded of candidates interested in NASA. She had planned it out in her head, the steps necessary to apply herself and the work that lay ahead to make her dreams come true.

The Ghost of the Girl Who Wanted to go to the Moon tells of her father summoning her to join him near the lake's edge. The Ghost of the Girl Who Wanted to go to the Moon recounts the shock when her father seized her and pushed her down into the lake's edge. The Ghost of the Girl Who Wanted to go to the Moon recalls with horror as her father held her face below the water's surface, tears filling his eyes, as she struggled for air.

The Ghost of the Girl Who Wanted to go to the Moon remembers the *tzitzit* of her father's prayer shawl, or *tallit*, floating in the water as she drowned.

As life left her body, he released her. She drifted from shore, face up, her eyes wide open looking at the starry night—and the brilliant moon.

It is a peculiar haunting, one of a young girl who dreamed of going to the moon, but is now trapped on Earth, unable to transcend Prospect Park where her dreams led to her being murdered by her father's own hand.

What is your dream?

Whose hand is holding you back?

Will you ever walk the surface of the moon?

The Demonic Wolves of Prospect Park

They prayed that Saint Francis of Assisi would save the people of Brooklyn.

hey are said to wander at night in packs.

No one knows where they came from. Many believe they originated in the basement of the Villa Litchfield in the 1860s. There are legends that the wolves first appeared as a consequece of the séances held at the Villa Litchfield during the Civil War. Other conflicting stories tell of the sudden appearance shortly after the U.S. entered World War I and news of the first casualties arrived in Brooklyn.

However they originated, the Demonic Wolves of Prospect Park soon dominated the imagination of residents who lived near the park. They could hear the howling in the middle of the night. They were subjected to falling prey to these ravenous predators, skilled in hunting down humans. Nearby residents feared entering the park after midnight when the wolves were said to rise and hunt in search of prey, of sustenance. Urban legends of the 1900s and 1910s tell of children that went missing late at night in the park. Most were believed to have been devoured by the Demonic Wolves of Prospect Park.

Contemporaneous witness descriptions of the Demonic Wolves are consistent with our own ideas of these wild animals. Consider how Barry López, writing in his book, *Of Wolves and Men*, describes the wolf:

> *The wolf's body, from neck to hips, appears to float over the long, almost spindly legs and the flicker of wrists, a bicycling drift through the trees, reminiscent of the movement of water or of shadows.*

This is similar to how Brooklynites also described the Demonic Wolves of Prospect Park during the Victorian age. Fear of these possessed creatures gripped the community. Tales of ravenous

Did residents of Prospect Park West and Windsor Terrace avail themselves to Saint Francis of Assisi to save them from these wolves, the way he saved the people of Gubbio from the Wolf of Gubbio?

Little Flowers of St. Francis, a 14th century florigegium compiled from the body of work Saint Francis of Assisi produced. In that book, consisting of 53 short chapters, Saint Francis of Assisi describes how he was able to reach out and, through his divine gift, speak to the Wolf of Gubbio, a possessed animal that had been terrorizing the town of Gubbio.

This ability to tame wild animals and nature, a consistent theme in Catholic hagiography, was evidence of divinity. In the *Little Flowers of St. Francis,* Saint Francis of Assisi writes:

Brother wolf, thou hast done much evil in this land, destroying and killing the creatures of God without his permission; yea, not animals only hast thou destroyed, but thou hast even dared to devour men, made after the image of God; for which thing thou art worthy of being hanged like a robber and a murderer. All men cry out against thee, the dogs pursue thee, and all the inhabitants of this city are thy enemies; but I will make peace between them and thee, O brother wolf, is so be thou no more offend them, and they shall forgive thee all thy past offences, and neither men nor dogs shall pursue thee anymore.

wolves from Hell terrified Catholic women who lived along Prospect Park West and in the Windsor Terrace district. These women decided to avail themselves to Saint Francis of Assisi for protection. Their hope was that in the same way that Saint Francis of Assisi had tamed the Wolf of Gubbio, he would intervene and answer the prayers of Brooklyn supplicants asking for deliverance from the Demonic Wolves of Prospect Park.

These hopes, encouraged by Catholic priests, resided in the

Saint Francis of Assisi makes note that, through God's will, the Wolf of Gubbio fell silent, raised his paw to him in obedience, and did as he was told. Once again, Saint Francis of Assisi describes the scene in his own words:

As thou art willing to make this peace, I promise thee that thou shalt be fed every day by the inhabitants of this land so long as thou shalt live among them; thou shalt no longer suffer hunger, as it is hunger which has made thee do so much evil; but if I obtain all this for thee, thou must promise, on thy side, never again to attack any animal or any human being; dost thou make this promise?

Catholic women of Prospect Park West and Windsor Terrace prayed that Saint Francis of Assisi would now intervene and save the people of Brooklyn the way he had saved the people of Gubbio.

It is said that Saint Francis of Assisi appeared in Brooklyn and walked into Prospect Park at a minute past midnight to confront the Demonic Wolves. It is said that Saint Francis of Assisi raised his hand and was able to calm the savage beasts. It is said that Saint Francis of Assisi engaged the Demonic Wolves. It is said that a deal was struck: once a week enough meat would be delivered to Prospect Park two hours past midnight on Sunday for the wolves. In return they would no longer threaten the people of Brooklyn.

The Arrangement of Appeasement under the auspices of Saint Francis of Assisi proved successful for years. Then World War I began. The number of men who enlisted in the army from the neighborhood was great. The number of fatalities was significant. Included among the enlisted and the dead were those responsible for securing the meat for the Demonic Wolves of Prospect Park.

The Arrangement of Appeasement struck by Saint Francis of Assisi that required the Catholic community of Prospect Park West and Windsor Terrace to provide half a ton of meat two hours past midnight each Sunday night was broken. This was a considerable amount of meat to secure in a time of war: it is the equivalent weight of an average-size horse.

World War I interrupted the ritual offering of flesh. The social upheaval precipitated by war was not a concern of the Demonic Wolves, of course. They wanted to be fed. They wanted to have their needs taken care of as agreed upon by Saint Francis of Assisi. They wanted their Arrangement of Appeasement to be honored.

Circumstances made this impossible. In a matter of months, the Demonic Wolves could no longer bear their hunger.

The howling began. The shadows—*appearing to float over the long, almost spindly legs and the flickering of wrists*—were seen once more in the darkest hours throughout Prospect Park.

That's how fear returned. That's why the Demonic Wolves are present once again. That's the reason offered for the slaughter of prey that is said to unfold in the imagination of a late night visitor to Prospect Park.

Are you near the park? Is it an hour or so past midnight? What was that shadow?

Did you see it? Did you feel the hair stand on your forearm? Is it chilling, to be out there, so exposed?

What do you think your flesh tastes like to the Demonic Wolves of Prospect Park?

View of Prospect Park

South Brooklyn and ✠ Bococa ✠

The Germanic Spirits of Columbia and Union Streets

The story is one of demonic design: the Sacrifice of a Child to appease the Guardian of the Underworld.

For reasons that are not well understood, an event occurred on July 1, 1882 at 111 Union Street that defies logic. The initial speculation was that something had gone awry in connection with preparations for celebrations associated with the Fourth of July. That was not the case according to two clairvoyants who have visited the location in question to understand more fully what occurred at this address.

According to police records dated July 1, 1882, Henry Luchsenger, a 12-year-old boy, was found dead at 111 Union Street. The boy lived there with his parents. The boy had a history of violent seizures, and it was presumed that in one such episode he thrust violently, inflicting mortal injuries to his head and torso. That is what the coroner concluded upon examining the injuries on the boy's body.

The truth is more complicated than that, however.

It appears that this residence—along with other nearby buildings up and down this street—constitute a gateway to Niflheim, the Underworld in Germanic myth. Bococa, the portmanteau for the Boerum Hill, Cobble Hill and Carroll Gardens neighborhoods adjacent to downtown Brooklyn, is an area of Brooklyn where many

German immigrants settled in the second half of the 19ᵗʰ century. It is believed that the cold winds that sweep across this stretch of Brooklyn are evocative of Germanic traditions. It is said creatures of Teutonic origin longed to extend their presence to these shores at this spot. It is said that there are several locations along Columbia and Union Streets that constitute a Gnipahelli, which is a cavernous passage to Niflheim.

Spiritualists who have tried to contact Henry Luschsenger report that they have encountered two distinct spirits present: one is a dark elf, known as a Schwarzalbe, and the other is a light elf, or a mischievous elf, who is an Elbe.

The story they tell is one of demonic design: the Sacrifice of a Child to appease the Guardian of the Underworld.

The Germanic and north European immigrants who settled this section of Brooklyn brought with them reverence for Germanic and Norse traditions. It is in this tradition that Hel— the malevolent goddess who rules Niflheim (Hell)— reached an accommodation: She would allow one malevolent elf and one benevolent elf to appear in Brooklyn, for a price.

The price? She demanded the soul of a young boy, whom she would feed to Nidhoggr, a dragon that devours the spirits of the dead, and is known affectionately as a Corpse-Tearer.

A demonic deal, but it was a deal nonetheless.

It was up to Schwarzalbe, the dark elf, to deceive the boy, Henry Luschsenger. "Dreams fill in your head," he whispered to the boy. "Don't ever cry in your sleep! Don't ever weep!"

The boy was enchanted by the dreams that raced through his mind, as beautiful as the sight of shooting stars over the East River. "You are translucent in your thoughts," Schwarzalbe told the boy. "Look at the shooting stars in the night sky!"

The Schwarzalbe spun the boy around and around. "Don't ever cry in your sleep!" he whispered. "Don't ever weep!"

And with that, he struck the boy once, and then again, and once more. Henry Luschsenger fell back, and he lay in the dark, with the smile of innocence across his face.

"It's so simple! The slaughter of the innocent is so satisfying!" the Scwarzalbe said, as he handed the boy's soul to Hel.

Pleased with the sacrificed boy, Hel opened the door of Gnipahelli, and allowed Schwarzalbe and Elbe to reside in this place.

"It's so simple! The slaughter of the innocent is so satisfying!" he said, as he handed the boy's soul to Hel.

Since that time, the western area of Bococa—roughly defined as the area between Congress Street and 2ⁿᵈ Place and west of Hicks Street—draws hedonists. One finds exuberance and decadence, where sexual libertines compete with practitioners of the dark arts, for a place to call their own. It is not without reason that Schwarzalbe is responsible for the sinister acts that take place in this area. And it is Elbe, a mischievous—but benevolent—presence, who is responsible for self-indulgence and hedonism.

"There are residents along this stretch of Union Street," one clairvoyant reported, "where men cavort in the nude, splatter paint on their bodies and roll on canvas to create art! There are places where Wiccans assemble to sow strife! Witches nurse from each others' breasts!"

The cold winds and fog that drift from the Red Hook Container Terminal hide everything, giving license to all. It is this freedom, with Schwarzalbe and Elbe as other-worldly overseers, which allows the cold, misty air to bear witness to depravity, hedonism, and confessions.

"The air speaks softly, like echoes carried upon the currents of the East River of the carnal pleasures that draw degenerates and libertines to these dwellings," one mystic stated. "But the price for this freedom— the freedom to indulge with abandon—has been paid."

This neighborhood, where Gnipahelli is hidden behind lives of exuberant decadence, holds a dark secret.

"There's stardust floating in the sky," Schwarzalbe told Henry Luschenger back in 1882 to deceive the young boy. "Look, look up at the star-filled night sky!"

In his innocence, he looked up. In so doing, he made it possible for other generations also to look up at the star-filled night sky and wonder in delight, amid the wine, cannabis, sex and excess.

"Whatever happens, happens in total forgiveness: It has been purchased with the soul of a 12-year-old boy whose life was seized on a summer day in 1882," Elbe confessed to one mystic. "There is nothing in this domain but sensual pleasure and the dark arts!"

There are only hedonists along this stretch of Union Street.

Can you imagine the pleasures of delight that take place behind closed doors?

The Ghost of the Cat Killer of Columbia Street

e lived at 140 Columbia Street, an address that no longer exists. He was a madman by all accounts. His name was Carl Soglow. He was born in Berlin, but arrived in the United States in 1876. He was proud to call himself a *Deutschamerikaner*—a German-American.

He distinguished himself in the field of engineering, civil engineering, and was respected for his intellect and work ethic. Then something peculiar began to happen as the years unfolded. Carl Soglow claimed there was something amiss in the neighborhood. He claimed that he felt the "unleashing" of Germanic spirits in the environs. He claimed to sense the excitable presence of evil elves of German folklore. He described a cold sensation familiar to those who believe they are near Gnipahelli, the mythological entrance to the Underworld in the Germanic tradition. He reported an unnatural abundance of cats in the neighborhood, boding ill.

Some say he grew obsessed with cats. Others believe he was intent on protecting Brooklyn from the dangers of evil creatures that were making their way from Europe. A few believe he developed an inexplicable case of ailurophobia, which is the irrational fear of cats.

What is not in dispute is that, by his own account, he read and re-read Edgar Allan Poe's story, *The Black Cat*. In his journal—part of his learning the English language—Carl Soglow practiced his calligraphy by

Some believe he died of exposure. Others believe he was poisoned by a cat-lover.

> *I approached and saw, as if graven in bas relief upon the white surface, the figure of a gigantic cat. The impression was given with an accuracy truly marvelous. There was a rope about the animal's neck.*
>
> *When I first beheld this apparition - for I could scarcely regard it as less - my wonder and my terror were extreme. But at length reflection came to my aid. The cat, I remembered, had been hung in a garden adjacent to the house. Upon the alarm of fire, this garden had been immediately filled by the crowd - by some one of whom the animal must have been cut from the tree and thrown, through an open window, into my chamber.*
>
> *This had probably been done with the view of arousing me from sleep. The falling of other walls had compressed the victim of my cruelty into the substance of the freshly-spread plaster; the lime of which, with the flames, and the ammonia from the carcass, had then accomplished the portraiture as I saw it.*

copying the same passages from that story over and over again (above).

It is then that he went mad.

Carl Soglow learned the fundamentals of taxidermy during the summer of 1890. He became convinced that the cats of Brooklyn were under the spell of Hel, the Germanic goddess who rules over Hell. He began to capture cats, slaughter them, and pose their bodies as if hung on a clothesline. He created a macabre taxidermy installation of slain cats in his house.

In the 1880s and 1890s his collection grew to number in the hundreds of cats. He filled every room in his home with the desiccated remains of these feline corpses. All the while he claimed he was trying to prevent the establishment of a Gnipahelli in Brooklyn, lest creatures from Hell enter the borough.

He grew more adamant on his need to seize the cats in the area. They were the Fallen Angel Lucifer's familiars, he claimed. He had become, among his neighbors, a deranged figure, the object of derision. Neighborhood children taunted him.

The ghost of Carl Soglow claims he slaughtered cats to protect the people of Brooklyn from evil spirits from Germanic mythology

No one was surprised when his lifeless body was found near Degraw and Tiffany Streets on October 21, 1897. He had set up an elaborate trap to capture stray cats in an alley near that intersection. Some believe he died of exposure. Others believe he was poisoned by a cat-lover. A few maintain he was killed by a Schwarzalbe who was intent on establishing his domain in this part of Brooklyn.

What is not indispute is that, upon searching his residence, the police found more than 1,400 taxidermy cats crammed in every room of his home. They found stacks of books and writings about the Germanic Underworld.

Since then, there have been reports of a ghost carrying a rope with a hanged cat. He wanders the streets, waving the desiccated cat while saying "Schwarzalbe! Verlassen Sie diesen Ort!

Verlassen Sie diesen Ort!"

"Leave this place, Scwarzalbe!" he implores across the ages.

Have you seen this Germanic ghost in the area? If you have, you are one of many!

Alas, this is the fate of Carl Soglow, who sailed to America for a better life. He did find a better life.

He also found madness, and a peculiar afterlife.

The neighborhood of Carl Soglow. His residence–140 Columbia Street– no longer exists.

He grew more adamant on his need to seize the cats in the area. They were the Fallen Angel Lucifer's familiars, he claimed.

He had become, among his neighbors, a deranged figure, the object of derision.

The Spirits of the Naked Hirsute Dancing Men

The building stood at 286 Columbia, but it is an empty lot today. The building was the house of men who worked hard, and who championed their manhood. These were men who enjoyed each other's company in a life-affirming arena of masculinity.

It had nothing to do with homosexuality. It had everything to do with what today is known as the mythopoetic men's movement.

What is that you ask?

This is a philosophy that rebels against the burden modern American life places on the lives of men. Specifically, it is a rejection of the idea that:

- *Men, rather than celebrate their masculinity, have become mere competitors in the workplace;*

- *Men spend more time in the domestic realm with women sharing household chores rather than with other men in non-work, non-competitive activities;*

- *Men, through work and domestic obligations, are unable to spend time with their sons, and thus unable to initiate them into the joys and responsibilities of manhood;*

- *Men are not allowed to express their emotions, especially around other men who are, in essence, their brothers.*

At the time when this household existed, however, it was odd for men to feel the need to establish a communal household where men found

The spirits strip naked and dance in the rain on the rooftops of the buildings along Columbia Street.

solace and strength in the company of other men.

They had certain rules. They let their beards grow. They worked with their hands. They treated each other as brothers. They ate meat, drank liquor and protected the weak, women and children.

The residence, a sort of free-wheeling fraternity house for adult males, occupied the second and third floors of the building. The first floor and basement housed a saloon. The affirmation of brotherhood in this household was such that men from all walks of life, almost as if embracing their inner manhood, were drawn to the place.

At times there were unforseen results. Police Officers Edward Cahill and Joseph McMahon, for

instance, were fined one day's pay on September 1, 1885 for dereliction of duty. The officers, while on duty, enjoyed a few beers and sang songs in the

saloon. Then they went upstairs, stripped to the waists in order to compete in arm-wrestling contests for shots of whiskey. The Police Commissioner took a dim view of such activities.

Newspaper accounts also detail frequent run-ins with the law by some of the men who lived there. On May 11, 1897, for instance, William McGarry was citied when 31 cases of liquor, enough gin to make 9,000 cocktails, were seized by the authorities. Mr. McGarry, then aged 38 years, described himself as a "speculator," the equivalent of being an entrepreneur in our own age. "Is this Smuggled Gin?" the *Brooklyn Daily Eagle* newspaper declared in its headline to the good people of Brooklyn. Alas, after more than a century, public records still document the "Animal House" antics that took place at this address.

Indeed, that was the kind of place that this place was: A residence of brooding eyed, hard-drinking superannuated juvenile delinquents who delighted in grooming their beards and moustaches, singing bawdy songs and indulging in drink.

The neighborhood enouraged this lifestyle. Younger men, working class employees with little education who had to work to support their parents and siblings, were abundant in the area. On 70 Columbia Street, for instance, a cork factory employed hundreds of single men. Almost next door, a Turkish Bath operated (Men's hours, 9 a.m. to 9 p.m.; and Ladies hours, 9 a.m. to 5 p.m.). At 242 Columbia one found a "domestic shop," where women were employed professionally to launder, iron, mend and carry out domestic duties that mothers and sisters would otherwise provide to unmarried sons and brothers.

The closest thing that exists in Brooklyn today to the Spirits of the Naked Hirsute Dancing Men is, believe it or not, the FDNY. A firehouse is also a community of men who live together, engaged in activities that are affirmations of masculinity and brotherhood. These are men who, voluntarily, remove themselves from the company of women for the duration of their work week.

The men who lived at 286 Columbia Street in the 1870s, 1880s and 1890s resembled the characters in the short stories Ernest Heminway published in *Men Without Women* in 1927.

Decades before Hemingway and almost a century before the modern FDNY existed in its current institutional form, however, these men had a weekly ritual: they would celebrate on the roof of their building, holding a barbecue and drinking, with magnificent views of Lower Manhattan in the distance. There they were away from the street (and the disapproving eye of neighborhood police officers). Beer, whiskey and their clandestine gin could flow freely as they feasted on meat-and-potato cookouts.

Over the years, in the natural order of things, the men would move out upon securing

CALLED TO ACCOUNT.

Policemen Charged With Neglect of Duty.

Commissioner Partridge passed sentence upon the following delinquent policemen this morning:

Officers Edward Cahill and Joseph McMahon, of the Eleventh, for being off post in a saloon at 286 Columbia street, were fined one day's pay each. Officer John Fox, of the Eleventh, was charged with using abusive language toward Miss Ettie Taft, who keeps a variety store at 258 Columbia street. Mr. Fox's proficiency in profane language cost him two days' pay.

Edward McDonald, of the Eighth, was fined three days' pay for walking with citizens, and Robert Barker, of the same precinct, was mulcted in a like sum for spending the time in talking to female acquaintances which he owed to the city.

Officer Cassius R. Stevens, of the Fourth, who was formerly in the employ of the Excise League, and who was appointed on the force last July, was charged with allowing a prisoner to escape and also with firing his pistol on Ryerson street without just cause. He was fined two days' pay.

marriage. Most would return on weeknights or weekends to enjoy the camaraderie of their brotherhood. Some of the men never married. They lived and died in this household. It is said their spirits dance in the rain.

The spirits strip naked and dance in the rain on the rooftops of the buildings along Columbia Street, between Union and Summit Streets. They sing. They dance. They are heard to repeat an anthem that has become the

inspiration to the men living in the neighborhood:

We will not become addicted to a worldly kind of sadness

We will not lose our masculinity

We are brothers in arms.

There is disagreement among clairvoyants about the number of spirits. One can make out five spirits. Another believes there are six. Only two of the spirits have identified themselves: William McGarry, the self-described speculator, and Joseph Donovan, who identifies himself as a distiller of fine spirits and a connoisseur of fine women. The men claim that they strip naked and dance in the rain because that's the only time they are free to shower. (The men of 286 Columbia Street found the confines of traditional bathtubs uncomfortable and the fees at the Turkish Bath too prohibitive for more than an occasional indulgence.) Now in the afterlife, they are freed of these considerations.

Can you make them out through the rain and fog on the rooftops of the buildings along Columbia Street? Can you see the spirits of the Naked Hirsute Dancing Men in the rain?

Do they look like something Robert Bly or Michael Alan Messner would organize on a men's movement camping trip in the wilderness of the Catskills?

Do they make you want to rip your clothes off and dance in the rain?

Do they make you long for the camaraderie that men can share with each other when they are liberated from the misandry that informs today's New York?

If the spirits of the Naked Hirsute Dancing Men inspire you to embrace your masculinity, then you will never drink alone.

The Soul of the Submissive Muslim

ome say it happened at 150 Sackett Street. Others insist it was 156 Sackett Street. It makes little difference. What is certain, however, is that it occurred on Sackett Street between Columbia and Hicks Streets. And it happened in

Sackett Street was a place possessed by a sense of freedom and an intoxicating aura of hedonism.

moment. These are the angels that, in Arabic belief, are guardians invoked during the

God wills it. If the exorcism fails, on the other hand, then two other angels appear: Angel Munkar and Angel Nakir.

Why?

A failed exorcism results in immediate death. These two other angels are the angels God sends to question the dead. If they are satisfied with the answers to their queries, they summon the Angel Ridwan who is responsible for Jannah, or Paradise. The soul of the person then ascends into Heaven. If they are not satisfied with the responses, well, let's not speak of the consequences of such an outcome, since it results in that soul being confined to Hell.

It was the arrival of the Angel Harta'il and the Angel Hamwak'il, however, that caused alarm along this street. Who had fallen from virtue to such a degree that God sent two angels to perform an exorcism?

A short digression is in order before that question is answered.

Ali Nader was the first to introduce the pleasures of *Raqs sharqi*, or belly-dancing.

1898, two years before the 20th century began. That much is also certain.

The event that occurred here was the remarkable apparition of the Angel Harta'il and the Angel Hamwak'il at the same

rites of exorcism. They are sent by God to prevent a person from falling from a state of righteousness.

If the exorcism is successful, life proceeds as

It had only been recently that immigrants from the Arab world began to arrive in Brooklyn. They were few in number. Most people in Brooklyn mistakenly believed they were "Turks," a generic name for immigrants from the lands under the rule of the Ottoman Empire that stretched from Istanbul to the Holy Land. That may have been the common perception among the public, but the reality, however, was a bit more complicated. A good number of immigrants were Arabs, and Muslim. With them they brought Islam—and ushered in the arrival of the angels from Arabic folklore and Islamic religious beliefs.

Ali Nader and his family were among the first Arab immigrants to settle in this section of Brooklyn. Intoxicated with the notion of America, with its freedoms and its dangers, Ali Nader breathed in the hedonistic air of Brooklyn and made it his own.

Ali Nader had dreams, dreams of voluptuous women dancing before him. He had expectations, expectations that one by one the veils would be discarded. He had means, means by which he could pursue his dreams. He was inspired by the exuberance with which Americans—and Brooklynites—regarded the exotic pleasures of the culture of the Near East.

"It appeared to me that everyone in America had read *Arabian Nights*," he remarked in his journal. *Arabian Nights* was the first English-language translation that appeared in 1706 of *One Thousand and One Nights*. "I shall endeavor to introduce the beauty of *raqs sharqi* to my new countrymen and countrywomen."

Raqs sharqi, literally "Dance of the Near East," was belly-dancing.

In his youth, Ali Nader had heard the stories and tales that comprised the stories of Arabian adventures. He longed for the opportunity to make these adventures his own in his adopted land. He wanted to

> *In his youth, Ali Nader had heard the stories and tales that comprised the stories of Arabian adventures. He longed for the opportunity to make these adventures his own in his adopted land.*

have gorgeous women dance sensually before his new countrymen and countrywomen in America. He wanted to indulge his sexual whims with the complete freedom he associated with the libertines of America. He wanted to kiss a maiden behind her ear, and feel her breath on his cheek. He wanted to admire the beauty of the crescent moon, and to feel the moist air of the East River waters upon his chest. He wanted to breathe in youth and joy, and delight in the senses.

To be sure, tales of Arab culture and its sensuality were inspiring to the people of the United States. His first employer in the United States was none other than Thomas Edison. Yes, *that* Thomas Edison, the inventor who was a sensualist at heart. Ali Nader's exuberance for dancing women was contagious, and Thomas Edison was receptive to the tales Ali Nader told. Soon Thomas Edison was smitten and became enamored with the idea of women dancing as they slowly undressed before him. When Thomas Edison first began to test his new

invention—films—one of the first subjects he chose were of "Turkish" dancing ladies. In 1897 Edison filmed "Crissie Sheridan." This was followed by "Princess Rajah" in 1904. "Turkish" dancing is the subject of some of the earliest films Thomas Edison made!

Ali Nader, for his part, grew confident: Sackett Street was a place possessed by a sense of freedom and an intoxicating and inexplicable aura of hedonism. He felt free to outfit one room in his home as a private parlor for "Turkish" dancing. He indulged guests' whims, as they gathered to see exotic dances and the dreams of sensuality contained within the walls of his residence. There was the thrill of the exotic. There was the titillation of the dance.

"This is the purpose of my existence," he wrote in a journal. "It is what I live for!"

What Ali Nader failed to remember, however, is the nature of fate, the truth of the Qu'ran and obligation to submit to the will of God first and foremost. In the telling of the stories of *Arabian Nights*, after all, it is always fate that appears, as if an angel, through one unusual occurrence. This leads to another unfortunate and unforseen event. This leads to yet another, until the narrative returns to everyday life. Once the protagonist has surrendered himself to fate does the natural denouement, as willed by God, unfold. Each tale, in essence, is the retelling of the Prodigal Son.

Ali Nader had become drunk with the scent of hedonism in the new life he built in Brooklyn. That is how he came to be viewed by God the Almighty: *the Prodigal Ali Nader*.

With this explanation as background, it is not surprising

that the Angel Harta'il appeared before him late one night. The Angel Harta'il quoted from the Qu'ran, 002.097:

Say: Whoever is an enemy to Gabriel—for he brings down the (Revelation) to thy heart by Allah's will, a confirmation of what went before, and guidance and glad tidings for those who believe,—

Whoever is an enemy to Allah and His angels and messengers, to Gabriel and Michael,— Lo! Allah is an enemy to those who reject Faith.

"My hands are cold. My palms are moist. My throat is dry," Ali Nader is said to have replied, falling to his knees and prostrating himself before the angel.

"Surrender your will," the Angel Harta'il said. "Submit to the will of God. It is the nature of fate to submit your desire to the will of God."

With that, in a moment, hedonism was exorcised from him. But, having devoted his life to the pursuit of sensuality and excess, when the Angel Harta'il performed the rites of exorcism, it was Ali Nader's very soul that left his body.

It was a failed exorcism: Ali Nadar collapsed and fell to the ground. He was dead.

It is said that since that day in the summer of 1909 his soul wanders the streets of Bococa.

Is his soul what possesses you when you want to dance all night? When the sweat of your brow runs down your face? When you feel the the sensuality of your damp armpits release pheromones? When a single bead of sweat runs down your chest? When moisture dampens your loins and you feel a tingle of lust?

Is it the soul of Ali Nader that takes hold of your being as you become enraptured by the dancing the accompanies lust?

If it is, gentle reader, then remember that it is the nature of life to submit your will to the will of God.

On the matter of submission to God's will, one could very well build a religion!

The Qu'ran teaches one to submit to the will of God.

A Ghost's Prayers to Saint Apollonia

A long 5th Avenue in Brooklyn, between 19th and 20th Streets there is an apparition of a man. He is seen walking down the sidewalk, making the sign of

Why does this ghost pray to Saint Apollonia, the patron saint of dentists?

common knowledge, at least to most people in the dental industry.

The reason?

Apollonia was an early Christian living in Alexandria, Egypt. In an uprising against Christians, she was killed in the year 249 C.E. The manner of her life—and death—led to her canonization as a saint. This is how Dionysus, Bishop of Alexandria (247 C.E. to 265 C.E.), described her martyrdom:

At that time Apollonia, parthénos presbytis (a dedicated virgin, which is to say, a nun) was held in high esteem. These men seized her also and by repeated blows broke all her teeth. They then erected outside the city gates a pile of fagots and threatened to burn her alive if she refused to repeat after them impious words (either to commit blasphemy by denying Christ, or by willingly praising any of the heathen gods of the secular rulers). Given, at her own request, a little freedom, she sprang quickly into the fire, but miraculously the fire did not do harm her. She ended up decapitated.

the cross, and reciting a prayer. His voice is soft and low, and his words are mumbled. "I pray to you Saint Apollonia" is about the only thing that passersby can understand.

Who is this man? Why does he pray to Saint Apollonia? And why is there a feeling of slipping into a catatonic state when walking down this street?

A few witnesses claim the man smells of seafood, as if he were a fisherman or had been

fishing. He often pauses in front of 663 5th Avenue. He tries to open the window. There is otherwise nothing menacing about this ghost. Today, this is a desolate city block, with only Korzo, a Central European restaurant bar, to offer a place to ponder the meaning of this haunting.

There is little information that can be gathered about this ghost—initially.

Who is Saint Apollonia?

Saint Apollonia is the patron saint of dentists. That is

Her suffering by having her teeth pulled out or crushed

one-by-one is the reason she is the patron saint of dentists.

The ghost that haunts 5th Avenue between 19th and 20th Streets, however, inhabits a city block where there is no record of having had a dentist's office. He could not have been a dentist.

Why, then, does this ghost pray to Saint Apollonia?

To find out required detective work. An examination of city records reveals that a century ago 663 5th Avenue was a popular oyster house restaurant. The restaurateur was Charles Lockwood, who, by all contemporaneous accounts, was an affable man, held in high esteem by his neighbors. There is no indication that he was a distraught or unhappy man. The only suggestion that something was wrong is found in a diary of a friend. In it, this man records of Charles Lockwood the following: "Once more, after several scotches, he [Charles Lockwood] confided in me the following: 'I am my own nightmare!'"

It is a puzzle that resonated among authorities who walked the block attempting to answer a question that has eluded everyone since that cold morning in January 1893— when the police were summoned to 663 5th Avenue. What astonished the police when they entered 663 5th Avenue was this: every gas jet in the restaurant was on at full blast and the entire establishment reeked of gas!

It was all the police could do to dash about the restaurant kitchen turning off the gas jets, and open all the windows. And there, in the middle of the restaurant, humped over a table, lying prostrate was the lifeless body of Charles Lockwood.

He had committed suicide.

The act of suicide is an act against God, who gives life and who is the only one who can take life. This teaching is common to the faiths that originated in the Near East. There are severe sanctions proscribed for those who commit suicide.

But, as is the case where humans are concerned, all is relative. This moral relativism dates back hundreds of years. This is how Augustine of Hippo discusses the question of suicide in the first book of *The City of God*. His purpose is to rationalize how early Christian martyrs who freely chose death—suicide—rather than save their lives by

The authorities in 1893 investigated the crime scene and—under the law— found nothing extraordinary. They concluded that Charles Lockwood committed suicide.

renouncing their Christian faith were not guilty of committing the sin of suicide:

But, they say, during the time of persecution certain holy women plunged into the water with the intention of being swept away by the waves and drowned, and thus preserve their threatened chastity. Although they quitted life ... they receive high honor as martyrs in the Catholic Church and their feasts are observed with great ceremony. ... May it not be, too, that these acted in such a manner, not through human caprice but on the command of God, not erroneously but through obedience ... ? When, however, God gives a command and makes it clearly known, who would account obedience there to a crime or condemn such pious devotion and ready service?

In other words, even though Apollonia could have saved her life by renouncing

her Christian faith, but chose death instead, she did not commit a sin by choosing to die.

Some argued that this was suicide.

No, it wasn't Augustine of Hippo replied.

If choosing death is *commanded* by God, it is an act of *obedience*, not *suicide*.

Forget dentists: Saint Apollonia is also the patron saint of suicides!

Charles Lockwood avails himself to Saint Apollonia in a bid to end his penitence here on Earth. This is what authorities in the paranormal claim. It is said that to walk the street where he lived— and past the building where he committed suicide—is a form of punishment.

Is the haunting of this street by Charles Lockwood a form of Purgatory? What might have been the extenuating circumstances that led Charles Lockwood to take his own life—but which would not constitute suicide? Did God command it? If so, then why?

The authorities in 1893 investigated the crime scene and—under the law—found nothing extraordinary. They concluded that Charles Lockwood committed suicide, pure and simple. His ghost, however, lingers in this world. His presence is still here.

Why? What secrets does he know? Are there secrets the ghost of Charles Lockwood cannot tell? Are there reasons why this suicide is not a suicide?

Who might be able to cajole the ghost of Charles Lockwood, who prays to Saint Apollonia as he walks the street in front of his beloved oyster house, to reveal his secrets?

Can you?

Green-Wood Cemetery, ✠ Windsor Terrace & ✠ Flatbush

The Catatonic Gargoyles of Green-Wood Cemetery

 ver the decades many witches have assembled at Green-Wood Cemetery.

They are ghostly guardians, casting an intimidating shadow upon the souls of the dead.

They have come as individuals and as covens. They have come to cast spells and to recite incantations.

Do catatonic gargoyles dwell in Green-Wood Cemetery? Were they brought to life by witches?

One of the uninteded consequences of their presence, their assemblies and their spells is the awakening of the stone gargoyles that are carved on some of the cemetery's more elaborate and beautiful mausoleums.

A small digression is in order. Thirteen witches are required to gather together before a "coven" is said to have been convened. Once a coven of witches exists, their powers are increased. They are more powerful in a coven than they are as individual witches.

In the course of their assemblies, most of which are benign but some nefarious, they have given life to gargoyles. These fanciful and horrific creatures, carved of stone or made of concrete, were never flesh-and-blood. In consequence, they cannot become fully alive. Blood doesn't run through their veins. Not all are fully formed.

It is at dusk, however, when the sky turns from brilliant orange to cobalt blue and then dark, that they awaken. When they do, they are in a catatonic state. Their eyes open and they yawn, but their screetches are inaudible to most human beings. They can expand their wings and stretch their long claws, but most are still embedded in stone and concrete.

These are the Catatonic Gargoyles of Green-Wood Cemetery that haunt the burials from sunset to sunrise. They feed on birds that fly too close to their mouths, or small mammals that wander within the grasp of their claws.

They are ghostly guardians of the cemetery, their emaciated bodies casting an intimidating shadow upon the souls of the dead. Their presence intimidates the living and the dead. This is the reason the anguished souls of the victims of the Great Brooklyn Theater Fire of 1876, buried in a mass grave, are not here, but remain trapped in a

A gargoyle on cemetery monument

vortex where they perished: Cadman Plaza East in downtown Brooklyn. This is the reason few ghosts wander freely the grounds at night. This is the reason the cemetery is locked promptly after the skies darken.

For centuries, the dangers of gargoyles have been debated among Christians. In the 12th century, Saint Bernard of Clairvaux was one of the more vocal Christians to speak out against gargoyles. Consider Saint Bernard of Clairvaux's words:

What are these fantastic monsters doing in the cloisters before the eyes of the brothers as they read? What is the meaning of these unclean monkeys, these strange savage lions, and monsters? To what purpose are here placed these creatures, half beast, half man, or these spotted tigers? I see several bodies with one head and several heads with one

body. Here is a quadruped with a serpent's head, there a fish with a quadruped's head, then again an animal half horse, half goat... Surely if we do not blush for such absurdities, we should at least regret what we have spent on them.

There is also the widespread belief that, though they might be bewitched, the Catatonic Gargoyles of Green-Wood Cemetery are still capable of luring the young through their sighs. Their hoarse, erotic sighs can entice the innocent within the reach of their voices. Over the decades teenagers have ventured forth into the cemetery at night, and have disappeared.

Legend has it they were devoured by gargoyles. Legend has it their remains were spat out in such small pieces that only rodents were able to feast on these morsels, leaving no mortal remains of these victims. Legend has it that walking around the cemetery's perimeter at night incurs the risk of becoming entranced by the wails and sighs of the Catatonic Gargoyles of Green-Wood Cemetery.

Is it true?

Have the incantations and spells of covens of witches brought the gargoyles to a catatonic state of life? Are they a danger to mortals?

There is only one way to find out, isn't there?

Will you peer through the wrought iron gates at dusk to see if you are suspectible to their wails? Are you drawn to the hoarse, erotic sighs of the Catatonic Gargoyles of Green-Wood Cemetery?

The Murder of Ghost Crows

A "murder" of ghost crows are believed to descend on Green-Wood Cemetery at dusk.

They assemble from the four cardinal points. They land on the cemetery grounds of Green-Wood Cemetery. They cover the lawns like a carpet of black feathers.

These are the Murder* of Ghost Crows that haunt Green-Wood Cemetery. They gather after the skies have darkened. They are reminders of the sins the people of Brooklyn committed that day.

The Murder of Ghost Crows began to appear in 1840, two years after Green-Wood Cemetery was founded. At first there was tremendous confusion over the nature of these apparitions.

What was their purpose? Why were they gathering here, in this cemetery, every night? Then it was suggested that the

---
* A flock of crows is called a "murder."

answer was found in the prophecies of Al-Farabi, more commonly known as Alpharabius, the Muslim scholar who died in the 10th century and who is remembered as "The Second Teacher" of medieval Muslim thought. (That makes him the intellectual successor to Aristotle, who is "The First Teacher.") The prophecy in question centers on the symbolic animalistic representation— *through animals turned into ghosts*—for the sins of humanity.

Theologians in Brooklyn, Christian and Jewish, who sought an answer to the apparition of the Murder of Ghost Crows in Green-Wood Cemetery, concluded that this was consistent with the belief that there would be a reminder of a community's cumulative sins against God's laws.

Confidence in this interpretation was found in the Bible itself:

Proverbs 6:16-9

These six things doth the Lord hate: yea, seven are an abomination unto him:

A proud look, a lying tongue, and hands that shed innocent blood,

An heart that deviseth wicked imaginations, feet that be swift in running to mischief,

A false witness that speaketh lies, and he that soweth discord among brethren.

These things are hateful in the eyes of God. These became the Seven Deadly Sins.

The Murder of Ghost Crows is symbolic representation of the Seven Deadly Sins committed by the people of Brooklyn each day.

Their numbers reflect how virtuous or how sinful the people of Brooklyn were from the previous sunset to sunset.

After this revelation was confirmed, it was decided that Green-Wood Cemetery would lock its gates at dusk. There is fear that the Seven Deadly Sins may become manifest should people be allowed to wander the grounds while the Murder of Ghost Crows hold dominion over the cemetery.

Is the Murder of Ghost Crows an accounting of the Seven Deadly Sins? Is the Murder of Ghost Crows the compiling of information for the Day of Reckoning? Is the Murder of Ghost Crows a reflection of the sinful nature of the inhabitants of Brooklyn?

What is the meaning of this haunting?

No one, since 1840, has been able to say with absolute certainty.

Is one of the crows in the Murder of Ghost Crows present for your sins?

If it is, then, in which of the Seven Deadly Sins did you indulge yesterday?

It was decided that Green-Wood Cemetery would lock its gates at dusk. There is fear that the Seven Deadly Sins may become manifest should people be allowed to wander the grounds while the Murder of Ghost Crows hold dominion over the cemetery.

The Ghost of the Widow of Windsor Terrace

She was widowed at the age of 27. Her husband was 31. The year was 1918. He was killed on April 6, 1918, on the first-year anniversary of the U.S. entry into World War I.

They were young, and hoped to start a family. It was, by the standards of the day, about time they settled down and started a family. Her sisters already where mothers of several children. His own siblings were all parents as well. They had hoped that they would have at least two children before she turned 30. That was their plans, as they lived their lives in the modest, but comfortable, district of Windsor Terrace.

Their home was on Windsor Place, between 8th Avenue and Prospect Park West.

The news of her husband's death in the battlefields of Europe ended all her dreams and hopes. A melancholy fell upon her soul. She was forlorn. Her family could not console her. They looked on, impotent and unable to revive her spirits. They

Neighbors saw an apparition walking up and down Windsor Place.

grew alarmed as her appearance deteriorated. They were concerned at her mounting indifference to the future. They were worried as she ate less and the silences stretched into days.

When she went to church one Sunday, one of her sisters became distraught when she

heard her say: "Death has killed the dream I dreamed!"

Nothing could convince her to change her outlook on life. She lost her faith in hope itself.

One afternoon, after having missed a lunch date with her mother and two sisters at a relative's home, they returned home and went straight to her room. The door was unlocked. She was in bed. At first her sister thought she was sleeping. Her mother knew otherwise. Upon closer inspection, the women realized her body was cold—and lifeless. It is said she died of a broken heart.

Within months neighbors saw her apparition walking up and down Windsor Place. She would walk towards 8th Avenue, then return and walk to Prospect Park West, and turn around again. She would walk back and forth, without making eye contact with anyone or saying a word.

The ghost of the Widow of Windsor Terrace is also, on occasion, seen wandering the streets, making her way towards Greenwood Avenue and East 5th Street, where she stands in front

Every night, the ghost of the widow of Windsor Terrace visits this memorial on East 5th Street and Greenwood Avenue honoring those lost during World War I.

of the monument to the men of the district who gave their lives in the Great War. She is seen walking along Greenwood Avenue to Green-Wood Cemetery. She returns to the monument. She does this all night, as she quietly recites the rosary.

Years later, her one surviving sister recalled that memories came rushing into her mind as if it had happened yesterday. "When Ernest Hemingway wrote his novel about the Spanish Civil War, that's when I remembered my precious sister's death," she said. Then she recited from memory the passage that touched her:

mute, apart from reciting the rosary. She communicates in a staccato of impressions and emotions. It took four months to piece together the basic outlines of her life while she was living.

It is this haunting afterlife, one of perpetual melancholy that resonates throughout the whole of Brooklyn. It is the unbearable suffering of loss that captivates witnesses. It is as if the Widow of Windsor Terrace bears the grief of the lingering loss accumulated across the centuries, from the Revolutionary War to the American engagements in Iraq and Afghanistan, which wear on the people of Brooklyn.

> *It is this haunting afterlife, one of perpetual melancholy that resonates throughout the whole of Brooklyn. It is the unbearable suffering of loss that captivates witnesses. It is as if the Widow of Windsor Terrace bears the grief of the lingering loss accumulated across the centuries.*

Not a lifetime, not to live together, not to have what people were always supposed to have, not at all. One night that is past, once one afternoon, one night to come; maybe. No, sir. Not time, not happiness, not fun, not children, not a house, not a bathroom, not a clean pair of pajamas, not the morning paper, not to wake up together, not to wake and know she's there and that you're not alone. No. None of that. But why, when this is all you are going to get in life of what you want; when you have found it; why not just one night in a bed with sheets? You ask for the impossible.

It has been difficult for clairvoyants to make contact with ghost of the Widow of Windsor Terrace. She remains

The Widow of Windsor Terrace is a solitary figure, often seen along two streets in this neighborhood: where she hoped to live a happy life, and where she makes a nightly pilgrimage to mourn a husband lost at war.

What of you?

Have you lost a loved one to the senseless whim of fate? Have you ever wondered how you could on? Have you had to mend a broken heart, or cure a soul overtaken by melancholy?

If you have, then you can understand the grief of the ghost of the Widow of Windsor Terrace.

In that sense, the two of you are kindred spirits.

The Ghost of the Ravenous Cannibal

Imagine for a moment walking by a building where, late at night, one hears a low growling, rumbling and gurgling that is both familiar and odd. Imagine if, upon careful attention, one realizes it is similar to the sounds one's stomach makes when hungry. Now imagine if the low noise remeniscent of hunger echoed like an ominous threat in the night.

Is it true? The legend? The story of the Ghost of the Ravenous Cannibal said to haunt the basement of the Armory on 8th Avenue and 15th Street?

Known as the Park Slope Armory, the 8th Avenue (14th Regiment) Armory is the National Guard building designed by William Mundell and constructed in 1893.

It is believed that the basement is occupied by the Ghost of the Ravenous Cannibal. This is the ghost of a deranged man who has been present there since the late 1890s.

The ghost claims he first tasted human flesh in 1882.

The Ghost of the Ravenous Cannibal, who has communicated with mediums, claims he first tasted human

The ghost of the Ravenous Cannibal is believed to inhabit in the basement of the Park Slope Armory

flesh in 1882. He lived in DUMBO at that time. He read a notice about the death of a neighbor's child. It turns out that Matthew Cullen's son

died after a brief illness. The boy was Henry Cullen. He was 16 months old, and he died on July 1, 1882. The Ghost of the Ravenous Cannibal explains that he knew Matthew Cullen. All he wanted to do was offer his condolences to him and his family. Indeed, he would only meet Matthew Cullen's wife,

Ellen, at the funeral for their son, which was held at their home at 307 Water Street.

At the funeral the Ghost of the Ravenous Cannibal looked

upon the dead child, not yet a year and a half old. Henry Cullen looked as gentle as an angel—and as tender as veal.

Yes, it was a sick thought. Yes, he knew it was wrong. But he couldn't help himself. He gazed upon the dead child, and he did look tender as veal.

But was he?

There was only one way to find out. The day following the burial, the Ghost of the Ravenous Cannibal dug up the grave. The boy had begun to decompose; he had to be prepared in a stew. The Ghost of the Ravenous Cannibal settled on Blanquette de Veau (veal stew) accompanied by seasonal vegetables, organic and locally procured.

Thus began his passion for human flesh. And an unbearable sense of guilt. It was a gruesome descent into Hell, the relentless obsession with digging up the freshly-buried, the search for recipes, the desire for more human flesh.

It drove him to madness. It drove him to suicide. His own death was reported in the newspapers as "self-slaughter," a dramatic phrase for a self-inflicted gunshot wound to the head or torso. The Ghost of the Ravenous Cannibal will not disclose his name. He does not want his descendants to suffer should it become known their ancestor was a Brooklyn Cannibal. He does not want them to be burdened by shame, or to be ostracized for his sins.

What is obvious to the medium who has made contact with him is that he was, in life, a man of culture. He loves William Shakespeare's *Titus Andronicus* and H. G. Wells's *The Time Machine*. He also occupies his time by remaining current. His favorite films are *Delicatessen* by Jean-Pierre Jeunet; *Eating Raoul*, by Paul Bartel; *Ravenous* by Antonia

Bird; and *The Cook, The Thief, His Wife and Her Lover* by Peter Greenway. He doesn't care for either *Soylent Green* or *The Silence of the Lambs* or *The Republic of Wine: A Novel* by Mo Yan. All these works center on cannibalism.

He is very precise about vocabulary as well. This is what he wants the medium to report to the world:

Anthrophange: The scientific name for a cannibal

Anthrophangephillia: A person who derives sexual pleasure from cannibalism

Cannibal: A person who eats human beings

Endocannibal: A cannibal who feasts on friends and family

Exocannibal: A cannibal who feasts on enemies

Gynophangea: A preference for eating human females

Gynophangeaphillia: Sexual excitement derived from eating human females

Pedophangea: A preference for eating a prepubescent human child

Pedophangeaphillia: Sexual excitement derived from eating a prepubescent human child.

If words exist for these things, the Ghost of the Ravenous Cannibal wonders, how can they be abominations?

How can they be unspeakable?

He wants the world to know that though he is a cannibal, and that his stomach rumbles, he is

abstaining from devouring human flesh. He poses no threat to the living who roam the corridors and floors above the basement of the Park Slope Armory. He wants the world to be reassured that he has no hunger for those innocents that come play at the YMCA, even if they do look tender as veal.

And they do look tender as veal, don't they?

He wouldn't hurt a fly, the Ghost of the Ravenous Cannibal claims.

The Ghost of the Ravenous Cannibal is also quite philosophical: "Everyone always goes on and on about what they want out of life. What about what you want out of death? Life is a few decades, but death is for all eternity."

Who cares what you want out of life? The more important question is what do you want out of death?

Ponder that, gentle reader.

If you're like the Ghost of the Ravenous Cannibal, it's simple: A good meal.

Blanquette de Veau

The Ghost of the Melrose Hall

For centuries Brooklyn has been the home of perhaps the most enduring haunting in the nation: Alva, the ghost of Melrose Hall.

This haunting has been written in newspaper accounts for more than two centuries and remains the most famous ghost story in Brooklyn. It is only fitting that this book, which has assembled some of the most thrilling accounts of souls, spirits and ghosts believed to dwell among the living and the dead in Brooklyn, concludes with the telling of the haunting of Melrose Hall.

It is also fitting that the telling of this haunting include excerpts from the accounts that reverberate across generations of how the people of Brooklyn have learned of this ghost, and how the story has been presented to posterity.

There are several versions of the haunting. Differing details are to be expected of a ghost story that begins with a clandestine love affair, ends in death and results in a haunting that endures across the ages.

Here is one version, published in the *Brooklyn Daily Eagle*, on June 22, 1884:

Among these old time institutions stood the Melrose mansion, gloomy, deserted and surrounded by the superstitious dread with which tradition has clothed it. The hall, the only ancient dwelling of English architecture in Flatbush, was built in 1749 by one Lane. Its solid

This haunting remains the most famous ghost story in Brooklyn.

Melrose Hall

hand hewn timbers have withstood the wear of more than a century, and to-day the building is in a perfect state of preservation. The mansion is a grand structure, two stories and a half high, with old fashioned gables and wide weather boarding. No plan seems to have been followed, the edifice being an agglomeration of immense rooms, secret passages and innumerable hiding places. A massive oak door, double bolted and divided horizontally into two sections, opens upon a large waldscotted hall, extending the entire depth of the house, while in the center is a

fireplace large enough to roast an ox. To the left, a broad mahogany staircase leads to the rooms above. On each side of the house are large wings; the right containing the ball and banqueting halls and the left the dining rooms and library. Above the banqueting hall is the haunted chamber, around which the traditions of Melrose have gathered. Until recent investigation divulged a secret staircase, opening into a closet on one side of the fireplace in the hall, the only mode of access to the haunted chamber was through the small stained glass window near the roof. In this room the beautiful Isabella, subsequently referred to, is said to have perished from starvation. What appears as a handsome buffet in the dining room, is in reality a hidden door. The back moves by the action of a spring concealed in the panels, and a dark passage is disclosed leading into the slaves' quarters. Deep alcoves, formed by the gables in the roof indenting the rooms and narrow hallways, afforded ample means of concealment to those who wished to be unobserved, and all the apartments are connected by secret passages behind the panels and tapestry.

Beneath the mansion are the dungeons, dark vaults into which the light of day never penetrates, where prisoners were confined during the Revolution. After the death of Colonel AXTELL, a human skeleton is said to have been found in the dark cell, the frame entire, though the skull was fractured, probably in an attempt at suicide, and the clothing had long since moldered into dust. Such was the home in which the famous old loyalist lived and died. The haunted chamber has a strange story connected with it: Colonel AXTELL having procured the command of the colonial forces, moved into the new home, with his family, consisting of a wife and two small children, together with a retinue of servants, among whom was an old slave who had gained the confidence of her master. Just before the arrival of the family a strange woman made her appearance, and took up her abode in the secret attic above the ball room. The few who saw her described the stranger as a tall, dark woman of wondrous beauty and kindly manner. Her presence in the isolated room was soon forgotten, as no one ever visited the mysterious stranger, except Miranda, the faithful slave, who upon her arrival immediately took charge of the dark lady upstairs. The fact of her being there was carefully kept secret from the Colonel's wife, and the superstitious negress dared not mention her name above her breath. Thus matters went on for some time, when the colonel was unexpectedly called away to command a dangerous and probably prolonged Indian campaign.

For some unaccountable reason the summons filled his mind with alarm and fearful forebodings, and he resolved after the family was at rest to send for the fair prisoner, communicate to her his apprehensions, and persuade her, if possible, to return to the home of her childhood; or at least to abandon the concealment of her prison room, now that his arm was

no longer present to protect his guilty love. At midnight, their usual time of meeting, while sitting in an easy chair before the flickering fire in the hall, the secret catch was sprung, and the panel slid back admitting the dusky form of the slave, followed by the dark eyed Isabella, who at once took her accustomed place on the stool at the Colonel's feet, the slave retiring to a corner to be a mute witness of the parting scene, or to sleep, as best she liked. Taking the willing hand the Colonel kissed the proffered lips. After a moment's

pause, he said:

"Isabella, I have been ordered to take immediate command of an expedition against the Indians, who have again attacked the frontier pioneers, and in a few days I must leave you. Fate has decreed our separation, perhaps forever. I cannot, dare not, leave you here in your present condition, without a soul knowing of your existence except Miranda, for she might prove false or might die, and escape from that prison room would be impossible. Fly, I pray you, fly! Here is gold, the woman

For more than two centuries the ghost of Melrose Hall, Mistress Alva, has captivated the imagination of the people of Brooklyn.

will attend your every want, but you must not stay here to die."

Indignantly she spurned the offered purse. Rising with flashing eyes and face livid with suppressed passion, she exclaimed: "What! is this the end; is this the love you offered me; is this the reward for which I forsook my God, my home, my very self? Am I then only the toy of a moment's pleasure, flung aside, when the idler has wearied of his plaything? Offered money in return for all that woman holds most dear. Do you look on me as a mendicant, whom a purse of gold can purchase? Oh, faithless man, why, why have I loved you, followed you overseas, to be flung aside despised and paid? Cannot your affection stand the test of a few months separation, or is this a mere pretext to sever the relations which you have so soon tired of?"

"Be calm," he replied, "for God's sake be calm and quiet yourself, or we shall be discovered and both forever lost. Isabella," he continued, "you cannot doubt my love? What have you given that I have not dearly repaid? For you I have wronged myself, my wife risked my chance of heaven, and for you I would die Such words from you are cruel; once more I beg you, go. Death lingers in these fatal walls. Life and happiness may be found beyond the sea."

His entreaties were in vain; the weak woman, strong in her love, remained in the secret chamber—remained to die. A year rolled by, and the Colonel was expected home in a few days. With untiring zeal the faithful Miranda had tended her charge, and the lady wanted for nothing. Only a week before the welcoming

Alva revealed herself to Axtell, who was then living in Melrose Hall. He had a secret chamber built above the ballroom, "fitted up with all the luxury and comfort that money could buy," and hid Alva there.

feast was to be given to the successful commander, the kind old negress suddenly sickened and died, worn out by the strain of a hard life. She lingered but a day. Her last efforts were to explain the nature of the hidden chamber, but her warnings were taken as delirious wanderings and passed unheeded. Isabella wondered why the attendant so long delayed her coming. the usual time for the visit passed—she patiently awaited the coming midnight, but no Miranda. Days passed and none came to relieve her hunger. She began to realize her fearful fate and that the room where so many happy hours had been passed with her lover was soon to be her grave.

Eleven years later, on October 3, 1895, the *Brooklyn Daily Eagle* published another account of the same story, only now it is less dramatic, and Isabella is called Alva.

What accounts for the diminished interest? It could be that with the passage of time, the manic desperation of some Brookynites to make contact with the dead—the soldiers lost during the Civil War—subsided. It could be that scientific rationalism prevailed as confidence in the Industrial Age grew and people were less inclined to believe in Spiritualism. Séances became less common. Confidence in Ouija boards declined. Ghost stories, once considered "facts," were presented to the public as "traditional" tales of apparitions. Consider this retelling of the ghost of Melrose Hall in 1895:

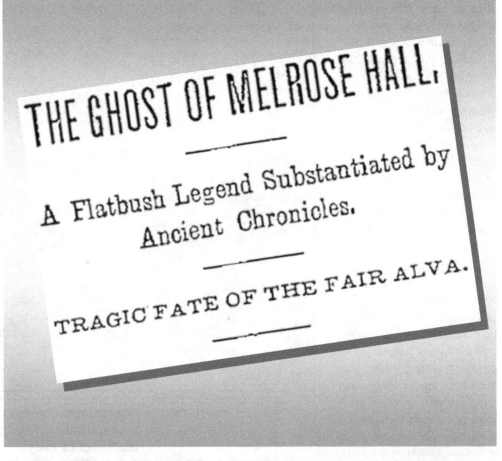

THE GHOST OF MELROSE HALL.

A Flatbush Legend Substantiated by Ancient Chronicles.

TRAGIC FATE OF THE FAIR ALVA.

Colonel Axtell, according to tradition, was the second son of an English nobleman, and he married the daughter of a wealthy British merchant. His fiancée was accomplished and prepossessing, but unfortunately she had a sister named Alva, with whom the colonel fell in love. Miserable, Axtell set sail for New York to serve in the American colonies, but little did he know that, "the next ship which sailed for that port from England bore the colonel's beautiful sister-in-law, who, as the story goes, had disguised herself by putting on men's clothes."

Alva revealed herself to Axtell, who was then living in Melrose Hall. He had a secret chamber (again with the secret chambers!) built above the ballroom, "fitted up with all the luxury and comfort that money could buy," and hid Alva there. One of Axtell's slaves was charged with taking care of Alva's needs, but no one else was to know about her presence. After three years of this unlikely arrangement, Axtell was called away for several weeks. During his absence, the slave woman died and, accordingly, so did Alva, who starved to death in her gilded cage. Mowatt heard about the grisly fate of Alva from her neighbors in Flatbush, who "affirmed that a young girl had been purposely starved to death in that chamber and that her ghost wandered at night around the house."

Six years later, when the *Brooklyn Daily Eagle* once again tells the story of the haunting at Melrose Hall, it is presented as legend. It is reduced to a simple pictorial display, with more images than text. The focus is on the macabre—where Mistress Alva starved to death after the death of slave Miranda—and the fact that her ghost is believed to haunt the area. It is presented as an urban legend, and the details of a clandestine love affair are discarded. What interests

readers is a public affirmation of the existence of ghosts, and the most enduring ghost story in Brooklyn. Examine, if you will, the newspaper pictorial, which was published on April 7, 1901. (The following year, when the *Brooklyn Daily Eagle* published yet another story about Melrose Hall, on October 3, 1902, the story is presented as a "reported" haunting, not as an unchallenged fact!)

What endures in the telling and retelling of this haunting, however, are the basic facts that are never in dispute. This is the ghost of a young woman who starved to death. She starved to death because the slave charged with looking after her died unexpectedly, and she was unable to leave the series of apartments to which she was confined. She had been locked away in the first place because her lover, who was jealous of the attention other men lavished on her, had her confined to a series of rooms in his grand mansion while he was away. The time in which this took place was Colonial America around the time of the Revolutionary War.

We now understand, however, that Melrose Hall produced two ghosts. The more notorious one is of Alva (or Isabella), who starved to death, and is believed to remain in the area where Melrose Hall once stood. This was on Bedford Avenue, between Clarkson and Winthrop Streets in the Flatbush area of Brooklyn. The other ghost, of course, is the spirit of the slave Miranda who is believed to wander Brooklyn dining in restaurants and cafés in order to find suitable sustenance for her mistress.

Of the haunting of Melrose Hall, two clairvoyants who have made contact with the

ghost of Mistress Alva sense her presence, but she is too weak from hunger to communicate much more than a few phrases. She wanders the blocks where Melrose Hall once stood. Not unlike the ghost of the Civil War soldier Augustín Vigil, who also died of hunger, she seeks sustenance.

Why does she remain where she does?

The ghost of Mistress Alva is afraid that if she wanders off, she will not be there when slave Miranda arrives with her meal.

Mistress Alva, alas, remains as helpless in death as she was in life.

THE END

✠ Maps ✠

BROOKLYN HEIGHTS

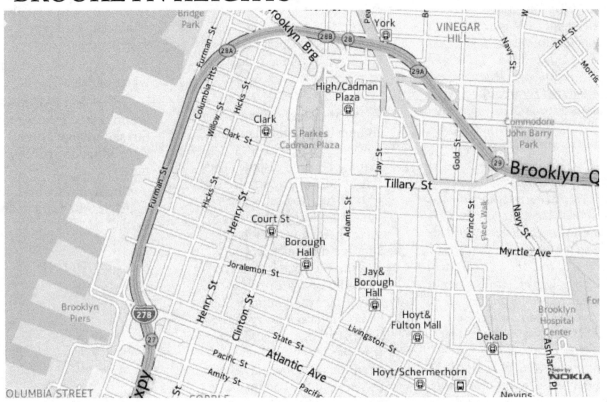

DUMBO

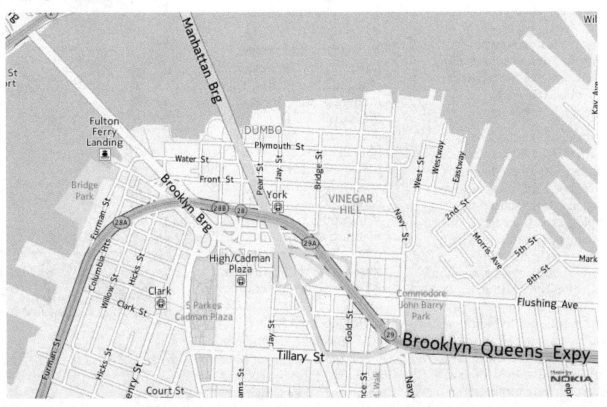

GRAND ARMY PLAZA / PROSPECT HEIGHTS

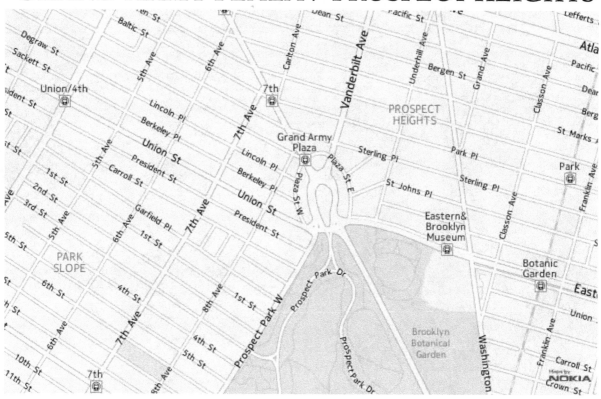

PARK SLOPE / PROSPECT PARK

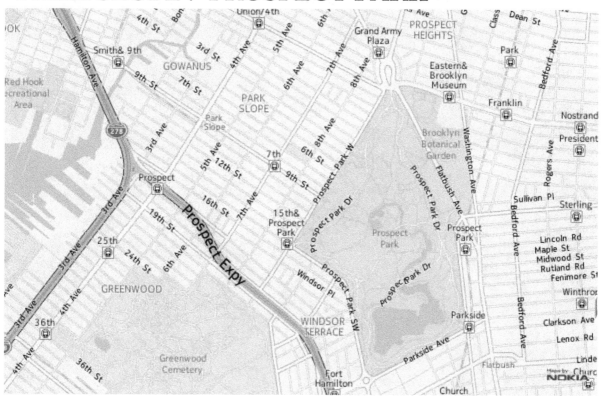

BOCOCA

WINDSOR TERRACE

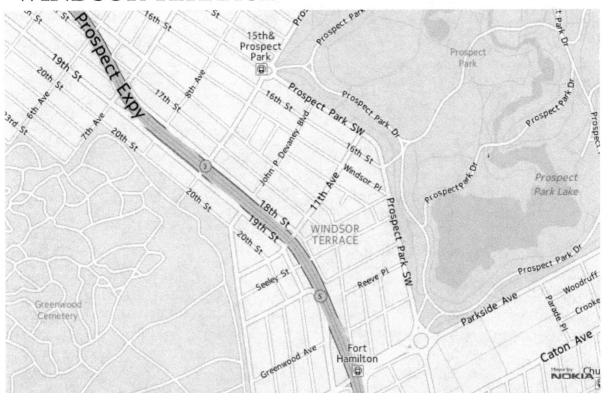

The Authenticity of ✠ Sustenance ✠

The **Spirit of Augustín Vigil** has been using Dream-Telepathy to summon authentic sustenance from Latin America. He has craved cheese, chocolate and distilled drinks. Following is a list of authentic artisanal gourmet products clairvoyants believe he has summoned to Brooklyn.

CHEESE

The most authentic artisanal Latin American cheese available in Brooklyn is **Quesos Mexicanos** brand. The spirit of Augustín Vigil covets *queso fresco oaxaqueño*. This cheese is available at three locations:

Quesos Mexicanos
2905 Fort Hamilton Parkway
Kensington

Las Conchitas
4811 Fifth Avenue
Sunset Park

Cholulita Deli
888 Broadway
Bushwick

CHOCOLATE

Forget Jacques Torres or the Mast Brothers. The most authentic chocolate is made from 100% Criollo cacao from Mexico. There is only one artisanal chocolate available in Brooklyn that is 100% Criollo cacao made true to the authentic traditions of the Maya dating back more than 3,800 years of craftsmanship. It is **Ki' Xocolatl** and it is available at these locations:

Brooklyn Commune
601 Greenwood Avenue
Kensington

Brooklyn Kitchen
100 Frost Street
Williamsburg

Chocolate-Earth
145 Front Street
DUMBO

The Chocolate Room
269 Court Street
Cobble Hill

The Chocolate Room
85 Fifth Avenue
Park Slope

Ki' Xocolatl is also available online at **Amazon.com**, or by calling **El Tri Market** at (855) 358-7444. Websites: ***www.ki-xocolatl.com*** and ***www.Mexican-Chocolate.com***

MESCAL (*MEZCAL*)

Tequila has been superseded by mescal. That's what the Spirit of Augustín Vigil communicates. He also believes the only mescal to drink is from Oaxaca and it has to be either **Ilegal Mezcal** or **Los Amantes** mescal. Nothing else will do when it comes to taste, pedigree and authenticity. To stock up on either brand, here is a list of Brooklyn retailers that sell the best mescals Oaxaca has to offer:

Borisal Liquor & Wine
468 4th Avenue
Brooklyn, New York 11215

Dry Dock Wine & Spirits
424 Van Brunt Street
Brooklyn, New York 11231

Gnarly Vines Wines and Spirits
350 Myrtle Avenue
Brooklyn, New York 11205

Juice Box
1289 Prospect Ave
Brooklyn, New York 11218

Michael Towne Wines & Spirits
73 Clark Street
Brooklyn, New York 11201

Nini's Wine Cellar
132 Havemeyer Street
Brooklyn, New York 11211

Prospect Wine & Spirits
322 7th Avenue, #A
Brooklyn, New York 11215

Red, White, & Bubbly
211 5th Avenue
Brooklyn, New York 11215

The Natural Wine Co
211 North 11th Street
Brooklyn, New York 11211

Uva Wine Store
199 Bedford Avenue
Brooklyn, New York 11211

Websites: *www.ilegalmezcal.com* and *www.losamantes.com*

— *Don't be caught dead with anything less authentic!* —

The **Spirit of Slave Miranda** has been visiting eating establishments throughout Brooklyn since the Revolutionary War. Here is a list of places she currently recommends for residents and visitors alike. Using a Ouija board psychics have communicated with the Spirit of Slave Miranda to confirm the following recommendations:

CAFÉS AND COFFEE HOUSES

Almondine Bakery
85 Water Street

Almondine Bakery
442 9th Street

The Chocolate Room
269 Court Street

The Chocolate Room
85 5th Avenue

Coleur Café
435 7th Avenue

Crop to Cup
541-A 3rd Avenue

Hungry Ghost
253 Flatbush Avenue

One Girl Cookies
33 Main Street

One Girl Cookies
68 Dean Street

Smooth
264 Carlton Avenue

GOURMET SHOPS FOR PROVISIONS

Apple Hills Creamery
623 Vanderbilt Avenue

Brooklyn Commune
601 Greenwood Avenue

Brooklyn Kitchen
100 Frost Street

Fish Tales
191-A Court Street

Sahadi's Fine Foods
187 Atlantic Avenue

RESTAURANTS

Al di Là Trattoria
248 5th Avenue

Applewood
501 11th Street

Beast
638 Bergen Street

Blue Ribbon Sushi
278 5th Avenue

Brooklyn Fish Camp
162 5th Avenue

Brooklyn Heights Wine Bar
50 Henry Street

Chef's Table at Brooklyn Fare
200 Schermerhorn

Convivium Osteria
68 5th Avenue

Five Leaves Café Bar Oysters
18 Bedford Avenue

Fonda
434 7th Avenue

Gran Eléctrica
5 Front Street

Henry's End
44 Henry Street

Luigi's Pizza
686 5th Avenue

iCi Restaurant
246 Dekalb Avenue

Locanda Vini & Olli
129 Gates Avenue

Mesa Coyoacán
372 Graham Avenue

R & D
606 Vanderbilt

Saul
140 Smith Street

Stone Park Cafe
324 5th Avenue

Stonehome Wine Bar & Restaurant
87 Lafayette Avenue

Talde
369 7th Avenue

Toby's Public House
868 6th Avenue

Vinegar Hill House
72 Hudson

Walter's
166 DeKalb

Zenkichi
77 N. 6th Street

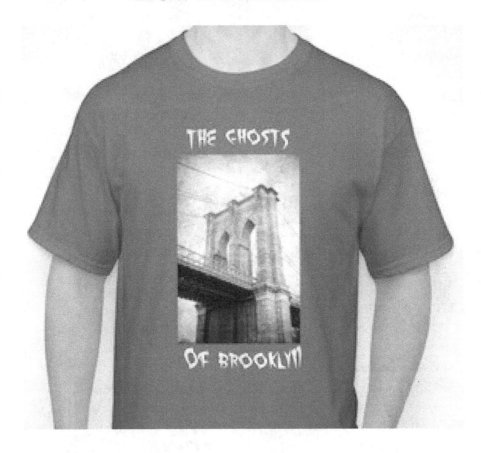

L. V. Salazar is one of the world's leading authorities on Fallen Angels and Demons. Trained in Spiritualism, Mr. Salazar has analyzed hundreds of sightings of spirits, souls and ghosts in order to ascertain their provenance and intentions. He is currently working on compiling a book about the ghosts of Washington, D.C. and San Francisco, California in addition to additional ghost stories of Brooklyn, New York.

He divides his time between New York City and Saugerties, NY.